OPERATION
H.A.T.E.

OPERATION
H.A.T.E.

by Richard Franklin

fantom
publishing

To all my fans over the years and over the world

First published in hardback 2012 by Fantom Films
fantomfilms.co.uk

Copyright © Richard Franklin 2012

Richard Franklin has asserted his moral right to be identified
as the author of this work in accordance with the
Copyright, Designs and Patents Act 1988.

A catalogue record for this book is available from the British Library.

Paperback edition ISBN: 978-1-78196-092-9

Typeset by Phil Reynolds Media Services, Leamington Spa
Printed and bound in the UK by ImprintDigital.com

Cover design by Stuart Manning

EYES ONLY

S.T.O.P.I.T.

CONFIDENTIAL

CONTENTS

CHAPTER 1
ALIEN ATTACK

MARTIN BIGGLESWORTH, KNOWN to his Army colleagues as "M", is a soldier and he lives in the North Yorkshire Dales.

This young man has many interests which include camping, travelling, art, architecture, history, theatre, film and politics, and he has a wide taste in music from the classics to the pops – though electronic "house music" leaves him cold: he told me he could see why people enjoy it at raves and things, but he doesn't class it as "music". Martin also likes cats, dogs – and horses at a safe distance! Cats particularly; and Martin had a very special one called Charles Tyrone Smith. You may think this is rather a posh name for a cat: well, it has a long story behind it which I might tell you one day, but it's too long to tell here for we have much more urgent matters to discuss! Sorry! Suffice it to say that Martin and Charles Tyrone Smith (using the stage name of Teabag for short) made a brief and famous appearance once in cabaret in Chicago.

To continue: Martin Bigglesworth was the Captain of the semi-secret Army unit known as STOPIT, and of course you know what that stands for... You don't? Well, STOPIT is the acronym for the Special Terrestrial Operations Project Intelligence Taskforce, the British Army's contra extraterrestrial-attack unit. This unit worked in conjunction with a Guardian of Time who had two hearts, one Professor Cosmos, whom they'd nicknamed The Brain because he thought he knew everything including all twenty separate dialects of Mandarin Chinese. Although STOPIT was a crack military machine, its philosophy was the preservation of peace and protection of the basic values of a free society – even if that sometimes involved the use of defensive force. You didn't know about STOPIT? Well, you do now – but keep it a semi-secret!

Come with me now, dear reader, and meet some of Captain Bigglesworth's colleagues who had gathered together for his final parting from their company, which took place on the concluding day of a particularly dangerous STOPIT assignment in which they'd all been involved. Imagine you see before you a very wistful young Army Captain parting from his equally wistful colleagues. Why was Martin wistful? Quite simply, he had been most unfairly "retired" at the age of only twenty-five (the youngest captain in the British Army) and it was not just his job he was losing, but his second family: and that is why his five colleagues were looking so wistful too – a family member was departing.

STOPIT, you see, was not only a fighting unit; its members were also very good friends, and the successful conclusion of this particularly dangerous encounter with the Seven-Legged Arachnoids of Saturn 7 had ended here, in the grand drawing-room of a great country house in the middle of nowhere, a couple of miles from the village of Checkendon in the Chiltern Hills. None of the young Captain's colleagues wanted him to leave the team, but the Top Brass of STOPIT had their reluctant reasons for giving him the push... but more of that in a moment.

It was the parting of the ways: the five who were now wishing him good luck and farewell (which when you think of it means almost the same thing) were looking very wistful. The Brain with his craggy features, wild curly white hair and commanding presence, looked glum; the grizzly moustache of General Hycock-Bottomley (known as the "Blustering Brigadier" until he was promoted, but now known familiarly as "The Bum") was fairly twitching with repressed emotion; and WO Bloggs, brave and brainless, "Smudge" to the lads, had his arms round Martin's two girlfriends – Joley "Dizzy" Darling (blind as a bat, daft as a brush and pretty as a picture!) and the cool Mary-Ann Peabody. The latter was nicknamed "Sniffles" as she was prone to emotion.

The girls were sobbing, their pretty cheeks wet and their mascara running like lava flows; however, Smudge looked as if he was more than content to be their comforter. Had Martin been less preoccupied he would certainly have raised an eyebrow in the Warrant Officer's direction and had a few words to say to him afterwards!

And what of Martin? How was he at this sad moment? Well... brave young army Captains in crack units don't cry in public... but inwardly a torrent of tears was welling up inside him. Still, even on that sad day of departure Martin found it in him to feel a glow of warmth at the happy memories of security, friendship and achievement with STOPIT that were passing through his mind. He reflected with gratitude how his original invitation to join STOPIT in the first place had begun in, of all places, the stalls of a West End theatre. It was the first night of a star-studded new play. By chance, pleasantries between him and the chap sitting next to him – a military type with a moustache – had resulted in his subsequent invitation to join the STOPIT team of which the moustachioed officer was the head.

'You're Captain Bigglesworth, aren't you?'

'Why, yes – how on earth did you know?'

'Your training officer at Sandhurst is a friend of mine; he was telling me about your excellent qualities. You're just the sort of chap we're looking for in STOPIT.'

'STOPIT? Wow!'

'It's the ultimate defence unit of Great Britain young man. High risk of course. Interested?'

'You bet! I mean, yes, *very*, sir!'

'Then come and see me in the War Office at 0900 hours tomorrow and I'll put you in the picture.'

That had been four years previously; now it looked as if it was all coming to an end. Wistfulness crept in. Every party has to come to an end and this one was nearly over.

STOPIT had always been a "four plus one" unit, the "one" being an ever-changing string of remarkable girls. Dizzy was handing over to Sniffles the following day but now, with the departure of Captain Bigglesworth, it was to be "three plus one". Upheaval time. Martin Bigglesworth would be particularly missed as he had been a full-time member through so many escapades.

And who or what was STOPIT's so feared antagonist? Well, he was a rogue Guardian of Time, also with two hearts, but both of them bad. This cesspit of evil was for ever trying to get the better of Professor Cosmos and take over the world with scant regard for humanity. His name? Well, the STOPIT team called him Moriarty because whenever he thought he'd succeeded in his evil plans, he would try and trick the STOPIT team into witnessing his triumph – and then eliminate them all at one fell swoop: just as Sherlock Holmes' antagonist, Moriarty, used to do.

Actually this is an interesting point: was STOPIT's Moriarty dead now or not? Everyone at this point believed him to be dead. While holidaying in Turkey, a vital component in his Time Capsule had exploded when, with Moriarty still inside it, he had parked it briefly for a photo-opportunity on the edge of a precipice... to be seen no more. The good world at large had breathed a huge sigh of relief; STOPIT though was puzzled that Moriarty's remains had never been retrieved – was he really dead...? and STOPIT always kept a wary eye out for the unexpected...

So why had the STOPIT Top Brass decided reluctantly that Captain Bigglesworth should go? Well, it went like this: on one of his previous missions he'd had a literally mind-blowing experience when confronted by one of his numerous alien antagonists. That particular piece of extraterrestrial nastiness had dazzled him, not with its wit, but with some kind of rare pink laser which had brutally stunned him; and on the next mission he had inadvertently threatened the life of their dear leader, The Brain, by sabotaging the latter's get-home spacecraft and confusing its Stellar Sat Nav (SSN) so it would plummet irretrievably down the first black hole it came to, never to be seen again. It seemed to the Top Brass that M's judgement had been more seriously affected by the pink laser incident than they'd at first thought. M, you see, had made the fatal mistake of trusting a bogus scientist who conned him into believing that his lab had found a way to create "The Dreamed-of Age of Eternal Bliss on Earth". In fact the band of scientific rogues M had taken up with (so nasty their minds would turn the Milky Way sour) were intent on nothing less than to harness the Seven-Legged Ones to weave their evil web round the globe and to entrap the Earthlings (that's you and me), poison them, and then take over the whole cabouche for their own hairy-legged pleasure.

Eternal Bliss? In hindsight you can see their claims were dangerous rubbish, but looking at the terrible state of the world today – all the violence, the poverty, the soulless, Godless, empty consumerist lives with no purpose that so many people lead – wouldn't you have done what he did and done your best to sign up to their vision? Of course had M known their real intentions – which he only realised at the very last moment when the Professor, who'd saved the human race himself so many times before, was about to enter the spacecraft he, M, had nobbled – M would never in a million light years have threatened his life. Blow up The Brain? No! No! No! What a preposterous suggestion! Of course he was no traitor! If anyone had lost their marbles it was the Top Brass of STOPIT!

Top-Brassy people tend to have the last word in this life, however, and it was not for M to reason why – it was for him but to do and die. So Captain Martin Bigglesworth was leaving... but he did, however, offer a defence of his actions, which would cast a dark shadow over future events about to be described...

Out of the blue he'd received an invitation, on headed House of Commons writing paper, from one Henry Archibald Thomas Etherington MP to meet him at the Athenaeum Club in Pall Mall to discuss The Dreamed-of Age of Eternal Bliss on Earth. In Etherington's letter, which came as a great surprise to him as he'd never met the MP (or even heard of him, truth be known – but he sounded pukkah), he complimented Martin on his bravery, honesty and idealism: all qualities he said he valued and aspired to himself. When Etherington had arrived at the Club he'd been immaculately dressed in a strikingly becoming black suit (obviously built in Savile Row). He'd looked very distinguished, was sallow of skin, with jet-black hair and eyes. A thin black moustache, as elegant as that of a

Douglas Fairbanks Snr, sneaked over his sardonic upper lip as if drawn with a surgical scalpel. In his hand he carried a slender attaché case of black calf, which M immediately recognised as having been bought at Asprey's of Old Bond Street because he had a similar one himself. The MP's initials H. A. T. E. were embossed in gold upon it. "Hate?" M had just smiled at the unfortunate word Etherington's initials spelt... he was an MP and what more trustworthy credentials could one ask for, than to be met by Henry Archibald Thomas Etherington, Member of Parliament?

(Frivolous and irrelevant thought: why don't parents think a bit more when they christen their children? As a kid Martin remembered some spotty little youth in his class who'd found a "W. C. Smellie" in the phone book, so he and his friends had had a great time pestering the unfortunate Smellie with giggly phone calls until their pennies ran out in the red phone boxes of that time where calls cost tuppence when you pressed *Press Button B*... and then there was that idiot of a schoolmaster at his school too, a Mr Pratt, whose initials were T. W. E. R... "Twerp"... the name stuck throughout his school career, poor harmless man. End of "frivolous thoughts" and back to much more serious matters.)

Mr H. A. T. Etherington MP seemed to be a great expert in Intergalactic Orientation Systems, and when he discovered that The Brain's system didn't have an automatic Intergalactic Orientation Homing Device (IOHD) enabling The Brain to return to Planet Earth whenever he wanted without doing endless calculations, and with always the chance of making a life-threatening error, he told Martin he'd show him how to adjust it for him... no charge! Really nice of him, Martin had thought... And would you believe it! Peace and Prosperity on Earth, which was The Brain's lifelong mission (for which he worked tirelessly and at great risk to himself, constantly being threatened by aliens who had their own selfish designs on humanity), was Henry Etherington's mission too!

They'd got on like a house on fire and Henry Archibald Thomas Etherington gave Martin precise instructions how he should "adjust" the Professor's spaceship. If only Martin had known those hateful initials on the attaché case did not stand as he said for Henry Archibald Thomas Etherington but were the acronym of one of the most feared and perverted organisations in our Universe – none other than that of Hyper Anarchic Takeover Enterprises... H.A.T.E.! Such a nice man the MP had seemed... and the rest is history.

As you turn these pages today you will find out how the threat of the Seven-Legged Arachnoids of Saturn 7 transmogrified into the even more bizarre confrontation of Operation H.A.T.E. The reality of the Yorkshire Dales where M lived, and to which he was about to return, was to prove the setting for an even more extraordinary mission than any of the STOPIT team had ever had to cope with in all their years defending Britain from alien invasion.

So, dear reader, it was goodbye-teatime-and-biscuits in the late afternoon on a summer's day. Distantly the church clock in Checkendon had proclaimed the hour of five. Pastel-coloured fritillaries were fluttering still to the gentle buzz of summer, and the chalky landscape of the Chiltern Hills, splashed powder blue and the scarlet of Flanders blood by scabius and poppy, shimmered peacefully. The silence was only disturbed by a final sniffle from Mary-Ann Peabody; efficient, unfazeable investigative journalist she may have been, but she wasn't immune to emotion.

The girls clasped his hands tenderly in theirs and they took comfort from each other's warmth. No one quite knew what to say. A touching silence. Then WO Bloggs skidded on a Persian prayer mat and dropped his teacup in the coal scuttle. The shattering of Crown Spode broke the ice: everyone laughed; Martin put his cup and saucer on the tray (without breaking it) and facing his friends he said:

'Goodbye and thanks – it's been great...'

...and he made for the door, the hall, his car and away.

CHAPTER 2
DOWN MEMORY LANE

IF YOU ASKED M now where he put his tea cup down or what he said to whom as he bade his friends of so many, and such varied, adventures farewell for the last time, he wouldn't be able to tell you. The confusion of thoughts and feelings that had welled up within him obliterated the details of his departure from his consciousness. Did he shed a tear? If he did he, for one, would not have considered this an unmanly expression of genuine feeling. His trusty little white MGB convertible growled fruitily as he double-declutched down into a lower gear at the end of the drive by the mansion's gatehouse and converted into a roar of release and freedom as he accelerated away up the country lane that would eventually lead him to the M4, M25, M1, M18, the A1(M) and home up the twisty, climbing B roads to his hill-town refuge in the Yorkshire Dales.

After his first acceleration towards his new life/old life, something inside his head said: *Slow down a bit M, do you know the name of this lane? It's* Memory Lane. *Slow down and remember, remember, remember...*

The car's roar subdued to a gentle purr, and the silvery-barked trees of the beech wood above Bottom Farm, his home – one of his many homes, the home he called "home" in the dark days of World War Two – emerged into focus now that he was going slow enough to see the trees from the wood.

So often during his childhood Martin would find himself wandering through these woods while his mother had cycled off to the aircraft factory repairing Spitfires, "doing her bit" for the War Effort. It was here that his independence, his imagination and his sense of loss were born. The trees seemed taller then, but they were the very same trees; the sun brighter as he emerged from the wood into the fields and chalky hills beyond. Here he'd wander discovering the "secrets of nature": he would search for the chrysalises rustling in the grass heads to which they clung; he would stumble on broken flints, and turn them over in eager anticipation that they might contain a clutch of amethyst crystals in their heart. Occasionally they did. For years he had treasured a fabulous one, at least six inches across: but sadly it had got lost on one of his many moves, as had Jacko his threadbare monkey who'd gone AWOL, along with the twisted fragment of a Nazi "doodlebug" (an unmanned rocket) aimed for London but which had gone off-course and exploded near M's supposedly safe haven here in the Chiltern Hills. These explosive events of the dim past were revived painfully in M's memory every time he handled them, and their loss around the age of nine had been the loss of his entire material holding. Memories of an age past.

This was an age without mobile phones or trainers, holidays abroad or video games; no sweets, no skateboards, no TV, no tikka masala, none of the things now considered a *sine qua non* by modern youth. Imagination and things you made yourself were the order of the day; the worst youth crime was scrumping apples for a dare, not knifing another lad to death for kicks… whatever had happened to the world of innocence?

The sign at the fork in the road ahead indicated Stoke Row to the left; M headed that way, remembering the terrace of little cottages where he and his mother had been billeted at one point: how he shivered in the tin bath in the kitchen… the smelly wooden privy in the garden… the dark and stormy night in this windy lane they must have travelled down in his father's Ford 10, the night of their evacuation from blitzed London… shafts of light emitting through the slits of black metal headlight covers… the uncertainty as to what they'd find at the end of the road…

A kaleidoscope of memories from a traumatic and nomadic childhood, which had set the tone of his life, though he only now realised it. For one thing, without a permanent circle of friends because of all the moves, this day-on-day existence by himself had forced him unknowingly to develop his sense of independence, his inventiveness and imagination, which of course had turned out to be such useful qualities in his work today (well, soon to be yesterday) with STOPIT. Isolation had also made him value contact when it was offered, though for many years he found his desire for close companionship was not matched by his ability to achieve it. Isolation had made him shy and not really a party animal even though he was instinctively a very fun-loving and humorous person. Consequently the value he put on the past three years with STOPIT was much higher than an outsider might have suspected: STOPIT was not merely a very close team, living and working together in good times and bad, it was the family he never had. The isolation and fears of his childhood grew rapidly into a questioning and growing confidence in his young manhood, and Martin's friends today are a goodly host indeed: of all shapes and sizes, old and young, dukes and dustmen. STOPIT was the core of his existence, so to have been involuntarily "retired" at such a tender age was therefore a personal disaster of serious proportions to him.

'Laugh and the world laughs with you – weep and you weep alone,' his mother had taught him from her own sad experience of life. In consequence M didn't do self-pity and he always thanked her for her good advice.

The engine hummed and M mused. Now on an A road, his speed increased and the past began to be left behind. There was silence in his mind but not for long… What next? You can never tell about the future, can you? Who knows what tomorrow will bring? He now had four hours ahead of him on the road to work out what he thought he'd do. In fact he was thinking so hard he nearly missed the slip-road that released him onto the first of the motorways that would lead him north to his hilly home in the High Pennines.

Middleham in Wensleydale (where the cheese comes from!) was Martin's safe haven, and he couldn't wait to get there; and lots of thoughts would float through his mind en route before his eyes would alight on the jagged outline of Richard III's ruined fortress. If you look at the map of Great

Britain, you'll see that this is the greenest part of England by far; and Martin considered North Yorkshire where he lived to be just about as near to Heaven on Earth as you could find. He selected a CD and played one of his two all-time favourite upbeat cheer-me-up tracks – *Hot Patootie* from *The Rocky Horror Picture Show* – at full blast.

This reminded him of a very happy weekend when, during a month's leave, he'd had to take over the role of the Narrator in *The Rocky Horror Show* in Paris when a friend of his who was playing the part had been suddenly taken ill. It was at the Casino de Paris in Montmarte and he'd played the part when he was at Oxford. In an inspired moment he thought it would be a nice excuse for The General and Smudge to see him in it and to make whoopee in Paris – and they did! Propriety forbids me to record the full gory details of that little foray to France: suffice it to say that on return to Blighty, Smudge had a hangover which lasted a week and The Bum has never stopped doing "The Time Warp"! M was now totally cool, and able to review his immediate past with objectivity. So he did.

Of course the first vision that arose before his eyes was that of his love-interest, the daffy Dizzy. Let's face it, she and M had been much more than close colleagues; and though little more than mutual concern and close compatibility in the field of action had ever been noticed on STOPIT's CCTV, a girl capable of such intimacy with an alien with a proboscis like a U-bend-plunger must surely have had more than a ballroom interest in one as eligible as Captain M! Dizzy was irrepressible, and wherever she was she'd be doing something crazy. Their special friendship had all started because of his cheeky inventiveness in making himself (and offering her) a cup of hot chocolate heated up on a Bunsen burner in The Brain's lab. Hot drink! Hot bird! And even hotter situations to remember... His descent by helicopter onto a Suffolk village green hadn't been too sweet an experience. At the end of that adventure a pint with the General in "Satan's Sitting Room" (the village pub), though pleasant enough, was a little tame when he remembered how he might have had a dance round the Maypole with him first. The General was a good man – no doubt about that: the very best – but there was a certain old-

11

fashioned formality about him that often made those close to him smile. If you like thoroughly mixed metaphors, you could say that under that velvet glove of a true gentleman's moustache lay not only an iron fist, but a heart of gold. The General had been like a good uncle to M, and feelings of military respect and private friendship were natural between them, but the boundaries were never crossed.

Now the General's love-life, however, had always intrigued his colleagues, for the former seemed more in love with his pint than his popsies. True, the unromantic name of Ada was whispered occasionally in STOPIT's corridors, but M found it hard to imagine that such a traditional figure could ever have allowed himself to unbuckle his Sam Browne in front of an *Ada* (especially as he was married to one Samantha at the time). True to relate, Ada had offered the General her timepiece once... it was even rumoured he wore cheap watches from his wrist to his elbow. The theme of the sex-life of his colleagues amused him as he sped northwards, so he continued this train of thought... now what about Professor Cosmos?

Did the existence of Professor Cosmos's dual-heart deformity enable him to handle two ladies at a time? From Girton or St Hilda's for preference one supposed... Mind you, his disconcerting habit of reconfiguring himself would make any lasting relationship a chancy business for any good woman wanting to settle down. Or was the Professor more interested in cross-dressing? At a STOPIT Christmas Party recently he had appeared as a charwoman, complete with bucket, which he claimed was a practice run for an essential deception in a master-plan he'd cooked up to thwart Moriarty: but everyone thought his disguise was rather too convincing!

Now Warrant Officer Bloggs was easy to fathom: no mysteries here! His sex-life needs either a sentence or a book to describe. After the Sergeants' Mess beer-up on a Saturday night, Bloggs (according to Bloggs) never needed his own front-door key!

As for the girls – what can be said? Martin realised he was going dreamy at the thought of Dizzy and Sniffles when he nearly hit a slow-moving hedgehog that had decided this was the point to cross the motorway, and quickly told himself he'd better stop this train of thought before he bumped into something bigger!

At that moment his penultimate landmark on the long drive home appeared at last on the road signs – Wetherby. His spirits rose to new heights for Wetherby meant horse racing; and horse racing not only meant home, it meant his passion, that great sport where kings and carpenters rubbed shoulders: that emerald grassy world splashed with white railings and the colours of the racing silks and charged with the adrenalin of the chase, the raising and dashing of hopes, and of course crowned by the steaming, glistening sweat and undulating strength and elegance of Horse.

Martin lived in Middleham, where through his maternal great-grandmother that branch of his family had lived for centuries. It was known as the Newmarket of the North – and horse-training and racing played a central part in the lives of one and all. Since the monks of Jervaulx Abbey had bred their horses in Wensleydale the thunder of hooves pounding on the turf had mingled with the tumbling waters of the rivers Cover and Ure. At least three hundred and fifty horses would be in training in this little hill town of seven hundred souls, and two at any one time belonged to M: a flat horse and a jumper – he liked the different thrills of both the flat and the sticks. His prize possession – well, he only owned one leg of it – was Glenugie, a wonderful horse that had been bred by an actor friend of Martin's who'd once made a TV appearance in a kilt on *Opportunity Knocks* and in consequence had become "Nobbly Knees King" in the Orkneys! So successful was Glenugie, so many races did he win, that he completely covered his costs – now that's an achievement, because most horses may give their owners much pleasure but in nine cases out of ten cost them a bomb.

M's mind travelled on to the stable-lads and apprentice jockeys who were his paying guests in his rambling grey-stone house set back from The Square. Formed out of the town's Primitive Methodist Chapel which was itself developed in 1836 from a couple of eighteenth-century lean-to cottages, M had incorporated the stables and a barn to the rear, and lovingly restored and created a rambling wonderful property, Hepple House. Beaky, Steve and Wac; Noodle, Nath and Take Away (the cheekily nicknamed and only Liverpool-Chinese resident of the town!) – they'd all be there to meet and greet him. The prospect of life after STOPIT wasn't so bad after all.

Middleham, you should know, is an ancient settlement situated on a nib of land some four hundred feet above sea level where Coverdale and Wensleydale meet. In years long past Wensleydale was known as Yoredale or Uredale after the river Ure which, swollen by the smaller river Cover, flowed lazily to and through York some fifty miles away. It is a very old landscape, formed millions of years ago by early shrinkage of the Earth's crust and worn smooth by glacial activity. These Dales have been inhabited and farmed at least since the Iron Age, some two thousand eight hundred years before the birth of Jesus Christ, and the ghosts of the past are ever present – not least in the much haunted Braithwaite Hall. Braithwaite, now owned by the National Trust, dates back to 1301 and was the home of one of M's maternal forebears. From Hepple House it is but three hundred yards uphill to the edge of Middleham where the Low Moor begins: crossing the fields at this edge of the moor to reach Braithwaite Hall the other side of the little river Cover is, especially in spring, an experience of true perfection. As you come to the river's edge you are stunned by a dramatic escarpment: at the opposite side of the water, little more than a babbling brook, and a mere twenty feet away, you are confronted by a rock face forty feet high caused by millennia of erosion. Brilliant kingfishers flash over the waters and wild garlic carpets its banks. Here you can't hear yourself speak as the spring waters, swollen by the melting snows of winter, crash and splash over its river's stone-littered bed. Lower downstream, where the Ure and Cover meet below Ulshaw Bridge, crossing-stones over three thousand years old were discovered.

The strings of racehorses on the gallops being exercised by the lads in the morning is a sight to be seen. Hooves thunder against the backdrop of the Pennines and if you pause, on the winding road that climbs to two thousand feet, before descending to the little village of Kettlewell, on a clear day you can dimly see the Isle of Man serene in the Irish Sea. The Low Moor at Middleham is dotted with gnarled may trees ancient, they seem, as Camelot; the curlew shrieks, the lapwing dives, sheep graze, and all you can do is wonder at it all.

M's car swung up the steep cobbled slope in front of Hepple House. The evening sunlight bathed the old grey-stone former chapel in a gentle pinkish light. He switched the engine off. He was home!

It can be chilly in North Yorkshire, even in the summer, and, after a Gin and French, we find Martin sitting down at a long dining-table in the former chapel with the stable lads enjoying an excellent "welcome home" dinner of lamb (put in a low oven five hours earlier by Mrs Spence, his dear housekeeper, and slowly roasting in rosemary since he'd left Checkendon) followed by summer pudding and fresh egg custard, all washed down with a tankard of Theakston's Old Peculier. Settled safely in an enveloping wing-chair that belonged to his great-grandfather, and with an Irish Whiskey in his hand, Martin felt mellow and in the mood to reminisce. Over and over again he went over the events that led to his "retirement" at the tender age of twenty-five. How unfair it had all been! How much he'd been misunderstood! He sank deeper into his Chippendale refuge...

But M had more resilience than that, and his mother's gentle voice came from nowhere: 'Laugh and the world laughs with you...'

'Brooding is for hens,' he reprimanded himself. 'What of the present? What action next...?' And as if in answer to his silent question the phone rang. He got up and answered it.

'Whippet Two?' queried the rich and plummy voice on the other end.

'General!'

'The very same.'

There was a click on the phone.

'What was that click? You still there, Bigglesworth?'

'Yes, I'm still here.'

The General continued: 'Just thought I'd phone to see if you'd got home safely, Bigglesworth. Apparently traffic very heavy on the motorway tonight according to the news. Made it did you?'

'Yes, thanks General: pretty reasonable journey...' There was a pause as M trailed off; the reason for his journey brought a lump into his throat. The General, his friend, heard the silence.

'No problems then?'

'No. No. All well.' But the General wasn't convinced.

'What are you going to do next? Got a plan?'

'Well, not really. Just relax up here a bit: do a bit of thinking...'

'Bad idea. Thinking always causes problems. Locate the enemy – take aim – and fire! That's my motto. Action, that's what you need – action!'

'Perhaps.'

'Take a holiday old man; pop off to Tangiers and get a grip of those belly dancers! Morocco – do you a power of good.'

The General's outburst was so positive it took M's breath away for a moment. Then he said: 'Do you know – I just might do that!'

A plan had taken seed. M put another log on the fire, recharged his thistle-shaped cut-glass whiskey tumbler, sank back into the big wing-back and considered whether he should take the General's advice. Half an hour passed... he heard the owl fly over the Square... the moon was rising in the darkening sky...

Then something very odd happened... curious, strange... the phone rang again:

'Hello. Martin Bigglesworth here.' Then a female American voice whined: 'You have a call from California.'

It was from Los Angeles and on the line was the Convener of one of the largest and most important WHITHER SCIENCE TODAY? Conventions in the USA, called "Fragilely". The aim of Fragilely was profound: it was to bring together serious scientists from all over the world who were pushing forward the boundaries of extraterrestrial and interplanetary research and knowledge, with the military and political hierarchy having to face and acknowledge the unexplained in the real world. Fragilely therefore would invite influential spearhead groups, organisations and specialist units like STOPIT to significant discussion sessions.

'Hello. Martin Bigglesworth here.'

'Hello Martin, Zac here.'

'Zac! How wonderful! Amazing to hear you! How are you?'

'Cool man – glad to catch you in.'

'Zac? It is you, isn't it? You sound different!'

'It's me okay Martin – just recovering from laryngitis. It's me okay. Hey, I didn't phone to discuss my medical history – I've rung to cheer you up with an offer... you must be feeling a bit down since you've left STOPIT.'

'Just a wee bit – that's so nice of you to think of me.'

'Now look Captain – we're holding a keynote Fragilely Convention here. Would you like to be our surprise Mystery Guest?'

'Wow!'

'How about it?'

'When is it?'

'In three weeks' time.' And then he mentioned a fee which couldn't be refused.

'I'd love to, but –'

'But,' Zac finished the sentence Martin hadn't started, 'the Committee thought that after your rough treatment by STOPIT's Top Brass you deserved a really refreshing break, so we're including a three-week holiday first so you'll feel fully relaxed.'

'Where?'

'Morocco.'

'That's extraordinary! The General's just suggested I should go there only half an hour ago.'

'Extraordinary! Well it proves that "great minds think alike!"'

'I told the General I'd think about it... As I've only just got back, maybe I could take up your wonderful offer and go there after, instead of before the Convention?'

There was a brief pause.

'We've bought your ticket already – it's a single flight to Gibraltar and after that a boat to the Moroccan mainland, and finally, if you ever want to return from the land of mystery, an open return flight from Tangiers. The Gibraltar ticket is already waiting at London Heathrow Airport for you to pick up!'

'What if I say "No"?'

'Are you refusing?'

'No!'

And that's how Captain Martin Bigglesworth's death-threatening adventure began…

CHAPTER 3
THE ROCK OF GIBRALTAR

CAPTAIN MARTIN BIGGLESWORTH was a young man of action, and a mere forty-eight hours later he was sitting comfortably in the grand *fin de siècle* foyer of the famous Rock Hotel, Gibraltar, with a large Gin and French (his favourite drink) in his hand... but he wasn't drinking it. Something had fascinated him...

It was a chic woman of a certain age, her blue-rinsed hair immaculately coiffured, elegantly dressed and smelling as if she'd had a bath in Chanel No 5; a devastatingly good-looking young man in his early twenties (if that!) was at her side. The two had just entered the hotel and were advancing on the desk.

'*Je vous en pris de registrer vos noms.*'

The receptionist was obviously impressed by this woman, whom he clearly recognised, and who looked a million dollars: she was actually worth a good deal more. He was clearly not unimpressed by her escort too, though that is not part of our story. She was well known to all around the Med, at all those exclusive spots that jet-setting celebrities patronise until boredom, and not the hotel bill, drives them on to the next high-class clip-joint. Her face was better known, you might say, than the Rock of Gibraltar itself – and if you're being beastly, twice as craggy! Her wealth was based on selling cheap goods to the mass market. Her "3d and 6d" stores (old money!) were famous throughout the duodecimal world; today she would be known as the Pound Shop Queen! What fascinated M even more was the shocked double-take of the receptionist as this easily recognisable woman of wealth was

19

signing herself and her young escort in under a false name: and the receptionist couldn't stop himself querying it…

'The state rooms as usual Mrs Hut…?'

The elegant woman cut him off (with charming abruptness): 'Mrs Bigglesworth.'

'Mrs Bigglesworth did you…?'

'Yes. Mr and Mrs Bigglesworth.'

'Yes, Mrs… Bigglesworth.'

'The west-facing suite: my husband likes a good view…' (the receptionist went purple in the face as he stifled a laugh at the thought of what view she had in mind) '…of the sunset.'

'Of the sunset, naturally, Mrs Bigglesworth,' he added, noting the stern expression on Mrs – er – Bigglesworth's face.

'Sporting old bat!' thought M as they disappeared into the interior of the hotel, with a flotilla of flunkeys carrying their matching Burberry suitcases. There was anticipation in her pace as the lift man bowed her and M's namesake, the twenty-two-year-old Raoul Bigglesworth, into the shining brass-caged lift.

Raoul Bigglesworth's name was on everyone's lips that season: he was a club singer and was known to his "sunshine public" variously as "The Voice", or "The Body" or simply, if you wanted people to think you knew him well, as "Raouly". Anyone who was anyone (and everyone there seemed to think they were someone!) had heard him sing and play; and anyone who was lucky enough had supped with him too: and there were apparently quite a few!

The receptionist caught M's eye, and winked at him. M winked back but regretfully had to finish his cocktail quickly in order to catch the last bus to Algeciras, the small town just inside the Spanish border from whence the boat would sail him over the Mediterranean Sea to his destination, the mystical Morocco.

M only caught the bus by the skin of his teeth and it was overfull with fat women back from the market, arms full of provisions, reluctant chickens resisting their fate, the wooden seats creaking with their household burdens, the armpits of their dresses damp with sweat. The gangway was replete with their unshaven spouses smelling of garlic and the red wine that they'd been drinking while their wives shopped. Order was manifestly not being kept, though the overdressed carabinieri, in their triform hats cockaded with black chicken feathers, tried so to do with much shouting and shoving but to little avail.

M had acted literally and quickly and had taken Zac's advice, accepting those generous American fans' air ticket to Gib. Zac's conversation over the phone in Yorkshire echoed in his ears on the rickety bus as it bumped over the rough Spanish road:

'...You fly to Gibraltar the day after tomorrow afternoon.'

'That's so good of you.'

'We love you!' And then the line had suddenly gone dead...

Before M had time to dwell on the strange coincidence that Zac's offer had echoed the General's Moroccan-holiday suggestion so quickly – almost as if Zac had tapped his phone and been listening in – his train of thought was cut off as the Spanish bus went straight into a pothole as big as a butler's sink. The bus shuddered violently, and M was rudely jolted back to reality as a big-bottomed Spanish signora with two chickens under her arms lurched into his lap; a great commotion erupted that was almost operatic with a wild chorus of squealing, clucking and raucous laughter. The carabinieri, who looked more like the cast of *Siegfried* than law enforcement officers, blew their whistles impotently, but did succeed in winching the chicken woman to a vertical posture on her feet. Decorum partially restored, M now focused on the journey ahead.

It's always good to have a plan, even if you have to deviate from it; indeed it's always good to be flexible and seize opportunities when they present themselves. As Shakespeare said: things taken at the flood lead on to greater... etc. You don't get good offers twice in life! In any event, M desperately needed a break from it all, and by giving himself the twin targets of the General's Gnaoua dancers (whose abdominal gyrations had clearly had some hypnotic power over The Bum in his distant youth!) and getting hold of one of those ancient-shaped amphorae of red mud-clay (in everyday use for carrying water since early history – and probably earlier) his visit to Morocco was given a real sense of purpose.

The sea crossing would not be a long one and, as the boat nosed out of Algeciras harbour to the open sea, the wonderfully refreshing salt sea air filled M's lungs – very welcome as he'd almost suffocated in that stuffy, bumpy, bouncy, noisy and overcrowded Spanish bus. He lay back in a deckchair in the bows of the boat and dreamt about his holiday ahead.

Suddenly a shoal of flying fish leapt from the water as the boat's prow cut through the swell and they fluttered silver, sixty or seventy feet before diving again into the brine. M watched fascinated for some time, but as the coastline of Morocco became more and more distinct, rising as if out of the sea itself, his thoughts were already leading him into the hills of Chechauen, the first stop on a life-threatening adventure of which he had, as yet, no inkling.

Chechauen is a pretty little hill town, stone and mud hovels clinging to its slopes in the sizzling sun. An hour's wandering had completed a stone-by-stone examination of the village and M could not resist the crystal water splashing sparkling from the village fountain. So what if the water was contaminated – he was dying of thirst anyway. For a moment he watched the locals assuaging their desire in the diamond flow and he reckoned it must be safe. It was in fact the clearest, sweetest spring water he had ever drunk, and he was grateful for it.

Tired and anticipating a long hot bus ride the next day, he retired to a little ground-floor room in a poor stone cottage he'd rented for the night. Full of sea air and happy thoughts he was asleep before you could say 'STOPIT!'

That night he slept soundly and dreamt peacefully: his holiday had begun... and so had the adventure of which he was as yet innocently unaware. Little did he know that another's gaze was already on him, watching, thinking, waiting. As he slept, a pair of jet-black Middle-Eastern eyes observed him through the slats of the shuttered windows of his little room, eyes of unfathomable profundity, and their owner was just waiting for the right moment to pounce. Moriarty was on his trail! He would follow M to his pre-determined destination and unavoidable fate.

CHAPTER 4
THE DARK EYEBALL

NEXT MORNING, UNAWARE of course that he was being observed, Martin arose and threw open the shutters on the early-morning sunshine. He marvelled in the beauty of the Moroccan countryside. The distant view of dusty hills sizzling in the sun was magnificent. There it was – freedom!

Already beginning to relax and full of joy, he was soon bumping uncomfortably on the next leg of his journey south on another local bus. Also full of fluttering, squawking women and children, clambering, yelling and getting excited over nothing, the bus bumped and swerved over potholes in the semi-metalled roads as before leaving clouds of dust in its wake. The day was already getting very hot.

Suddenly, round a corner in the middle of nowhere, a battered Army vehicle bristling with a clutch of scruffy soldiers brought the bus to a skidding halt at the roadside. Two unshaven and thoroughly evil-looking Arabs (who had been clinging to the rear footplate of the bus since they'd mounted it at a deserted and apparently unscheduled stop a couple of miles back) were promptly arrested and the brown-paper parcels they'd been carrying seized and opened. They contained .303 British Army rifles of a long-since discontinued mark. The soldiers made off with their captives and the rifles, and the bus lurched on towards the ancient city of Fez. It seemed an endless dusty trail, along dusty roads that wound up and up, and on and on through dusty hills.

Fez was fantastic! Massive mediaeval doors, carved intricately five hundred years ago, protected the great university building. Then there were the women washing newly woven fabric in the big stream that babbles through the city, dying material with bright colours from boxes of paint powders of vivid brilliance beside them. Blue, yellow, orange, green. Thirsty again, M wandered through the market. A young tourist bumped up against him in the crowd as he stood, dazzled and dazed by the colours, the noise and the exotic smells of this amazing souk.

'Sorry boyo!' said the tourist youth, 'it's like a rugger scrum!'

'No probs.'

'They could play it with water melons here.' They both chuckled.

The youth had a strong Welsh accent and M, who knew a bit about accents, recognised at once that he came from the region of Swansea.

'I'm David. You looking for anything in particular?'

'Just presents for the family.'

'Leather's cheap – I'll show you a good stall if you like.'

'Cool – thanks.'

'I've been here a couple of days,' said David as he led Martin to a smiling Middle Eastern selling leather goods.

'A pouffe – that's a good idea,' said M appreciatively.

'Poofs to you!' More chuckling and bonding. 'Enjoy a haggle,' said David, 'they expect you to and you'll get it cheaper. See you!' And he melted into the crowd.

So haggle Martin did. In the course of the bartering the vendor produced cups of sweet mint tea, over which the deal was eventually done.

'Where are you heading for?' asked the leather-selling Moroccan.

'Marrakech.'

'Ah, it's very expensive there,' the vendor claimed inevitably, 'my cushions are half the price.

'I like the colour of this one,' said Martin.

'You won't find a better one anywhere,' said the boastful salesman. 'I only use skin from the finest camels.'

The conversation continued – in French of course – and eventually Martin became the owner of a beautiful cream and pink and gold pouffe cushion which he subsequently gave to his parents and a leather folder in the same colours which he kept for himself.

As M left the vendor in his market stall and wandered into the throng, he was not to know that a man with jet-black eyes of unfathomable profundity had silently emerged from behind a carpet hanging in the stall behind the leather-seller.

'Excuse me. That young Englishman, buying your pouffe cushion…?'

'Yes?'

'Did he say where he was going?'

'To Marrakech.'

'Ah,' thought dark eyes, 'so that is where we shall meet!'

Martin, back in the youth hostel where he was staying, was well pleased with his first Moroccan purchase and by a wonderful bit of good luck found David staying at the same hostel too, so he was able to thank him for his advice. Martin packed the pouffe cushion in his backpack ready for a very early start in the morning (again by a bone-shaking cross-country bus) to his final destination, Marrakech. Then he and David went out together for a simple couscous and got slightly tiddly on a delicious local wine followed by black grapes and goats'-milk cheese in a backstreet coccina. They exchanged all their travel plans, laughed a lot, swore to meet again when they got back home and returned to the hostel.

'…and don't forget Mart, when you're in Marrakech you just *must* see the snake charmer!'

And tumbling into his bunk Martin fell asleep in an instant. It had been a long day full of new sights and smells and experiences and the heat and the travelling had exhausted him.

In the middle of the night, however, he awoke with a start: he felt he was trapped! It was pitch black and he could see nothing. Half asleep still, he couldn't remember where he was but he felt he must escape. For a second he panicked. He sat bolt upright hitting his head on the underside of David's bunk above him; then rolling onto the floor he ran until he found a chink of light from the sky. He was in a tiny courtyard within the centre of the hostel. With relief he saw the stars and the untidy outline of bougainvillea tumbling over the walls. Calm now, he crept back to his dormitory hoping he hadn't woken David and that his new friend hadn't seen his embarrassing panic attack... but David's bunk was empty!

'Odd! I hope he's all right.'

Quietly lying down Martin dozed fitfully until the cocks crew, then he arose and went his way.

But where was the Welshman? He worried for a while but the tribulations of travel soon swamped his puzzlement. It was getting much hotter here now he was in the interior of the country; it was to be his longest journey yet and he did not expect to reach Marrakech much before nightfall. He didn't mind – it was all a novelty and an adventure: perhaps he would have been less keen if he'd known what was in store for him...

The bus bumped across dusty plains not coming upon travellers of any kind for many miles at a time. In the middle of absolutely nowhere they stopped to pick up a fair-haired Arab in a fine flowing djellaba. Some miles on, no habitation in sight, the bus pulled up without command and the Christ-like figure descended without a word, and made off in silence towards the empty horizon to disappear into a haze of shimmering heat. There was a great dignity and mystery about him. No explanation.

Later, another mystery: somewhere in that sun-baked nowhere, he spotted a cage of wood within which two men were chained. No food, no water, gasping in the heat. Summary punishment for some unknown misdemeanour.

'More effective than the doddle of community service,' Martin reflected. 'Whatever they've done, they won't do it again.'

In the mid afternoon, excitement! An oasis appeared on the horizon. Half an hour later the mirage had become a reality. Martin had never been to an oasis before and now realised how welcome they could be. He was amazed to see a Coca Cola sign proclaiming the presence of that welcome beverage, and before getting back on the bus he wandered among the palms and tough-leaved cacti grateful for their cool shade.

Back on the bus and bumping at breakneck speed on the last leg of the never-ending road to Marrakech, M tried to open a little sliding window beside him for cooler air: but it did little good, as the air that blew in was scorching hot itself. Hour followed hour; the day got cooler as the sun descended towards the horizon. The bus had been climbing for some time and now it had reached its peak, and as it turned a sharp corner and the descent began, there, ten miles away in the distant plain, was Marrakech, basking in the last of the long day's sun.

Nearer and nearer, larger and larger. Now the details of the ancient city had become clear. There before him were the massive red concrete castellated walls of Marrakech standing impenetrable beyond a grove of, some say, thirty thousand palm trees.

The sun, a fiery red ball, was descending slowly to the west, setting the red walls afire it seemed: a fire without smoke. Now out through the giant keyhole gates of the city streamed the Muslim devout, facing Mecca to pray before nightfall. Camels moved with Biblical certainty, and as if in slow motion or in a dream or walking through water: a thousand djellabas swayed in unison in the gentle breeze. All became still. M marvelled. Once into the city through the huge gates, all was hustle and bustle again. The bus disgorged its passengers and Martin found himself surrounded by a rabble of urchins – no sci-fi enthusiasts they, seeking autographs from a popular TV celebrity – oh no! These were a hungry horde of poor little wretches seeking a coin or two to carry his backpack perhaps, or to eat a crumb that might fall from his table. One lad had the luck to be chosen as M's porter:

'*Je cherche l'auberge de jeunesse,*' Martin suggested with a confidence in French he did not feel.

'*C'est loin d'ici... c'est mieux tu viens avec moi. Je connais un bon pension: c'est fort bien.*'

Martin didn't argue and allowed the boy to lead him to the "*fort bien*" pension the boy had suggested: he'd probably get commission from the proprietor for leading him there, and anyway the youth hostel was the other side of the city in the *Ville Nouvelle* which did not interest Martin. He was exhausted and prepared to settle for anything... but when he got there he almost changed his mind! It was a truly disgusting backstreet kitchen with one letting room. It was so late now and it was cheap so he just had to put up with it. Clutching Martin's small but larger than necessary offering the boy ran off triumphantly: it would be food for supper for a whole family. M couldn't be bothered to go looking for food now, so he finished off an uneaten sandwich he'd made for the journey and washed it down with a bottle of (now warm!) mineral water he'd acquired at the oasis.

To bed... or not to bed as it turned out. As he turned down the sheets, it was clear he was not the first person to have been using them – nor the second or third or sixth! They were filthy! The bed was filthy. The floor was filthy. It was now too late to move so he slept on top of a large chest of drawers in the corner of the room. Luckily he was so exhausted he fell asleep at once. He never heard the floorboards creak, or saw the dark eyeball glinting through the keyhole...

CHAPTER 5
THE SNAKE CHARMER

THE SUN HAD not long risen when Martin opened his eyes on day four of his travels, and yes, he was slightly stiff from sleeping on top of the chest of drawers; but anyway clean socks, a pair of Calvin Kleins and a splash of water on his face and Martin was ready to face the world. Early rising and some discomfort was not a problem to soldiers or stable lads!

Little did he guess that it was now just a matter of hours before a surprise would lie in store for him – a fatal surprise. Before the sun had set again on this enchanted city of Marrakech, his die would have been cast. But who can escape his fate? All a wise man can do is train himself to be ready to meet whatever Fate has in store and Martin (as we know) was a wise young man. None of these thoughts, of course, were passing through his mind: he was just glad to be out in the fresh morning air. And who should be there, caught by a shaft of sunlight in a doorway opposite, but the urchin, Martin's porter from the night before!

Judah – for that was his name – got to his feet and approached M diffidently: would the generous Englishman be angry with him for hanging around he wondered?

'*Tu veux rencontrer ma famille, Monsieur?*'

Martin was touched by the invitation and was curious to see under what conditions people like Judah lived.

'*Merci bien.*'

'*Donc viens – viens avec moi.*' And with Martin's acceptance the boy raced off with his backpack. Martin was glad he'd accepted the invitation, for it was to be a first-hand experience with abject poverty that he would never forget and for ever be grateful for his own comforts.

The boy led him through increasingly narrow and dirty streets, in the gutters of which scraggy dogs and cats sought rotten food among the excrement of beast and man; where people in rags scurried on urgent errands for survival. It was a world of rats and cockroaches, stench and filth. Here a half-demented creature, human but on all fours, crawled in the road seeking nourishment, moaning, oozing his own filth: Martin couldn't believe what he saw. The boy led on; finally they came to a hole in a massive broken wall. With a smile of pride the boy said: '*J'habite ici!* I live here!'

They stepped through the hole into another world beyond, worse than the first: poverty compounded by social ostracisation. It was the "mellah" or Jewish quarter, and the Jews were outcasts at that time in an Arab society. He took Martin into the simple synagogue that served also as his school. Nearby was Judah's home which consisted of a very small square courtyard, open to the sky above. On the opposite wall to the entrance archway was an open stone staircase leading up to a narrow gallery which accessed four rooms: and it was in these four rooms that two families lived.

There must have been fifteen people of all ages in that dwelling. They all crowded round Martin now, eager to see this stranger who was probably rich... but neither Judah nor his family begged for anything. They just welcomed him, wanted to look at him – and Judah wanted to show off his home. He was proud of it: it had running water! Yes – one exterior tap from which flowed clean, cold water. That was status, for you didn't have to go to a public fountain. Soon the kitchen was in action and Martin was being offered a delicious savoury meatball, that emerged steaming from a red clay *marmite*.

The kitchen? Well that was four bricks raising the pot over hot charcoals, in the triangular space formed by the stone steps which rose up the wall from the courtyard to the floor above. Some of the woman ran giggling up the steps, dragging Martin by the hand with them. They showed him into one of the rooms above; in the centre was a huge pile of what looked like rags. It was their communal wardrobe – their Sunday best. They all selected scarves, vests and handkerchiefs and, proudly putting them on, indicated they wanted Martin to photograph them thus bedecked. After some awkward moments of smiling with little really to say, and some further grunts of appreciation and admiration from Martin (they were so proud of their paltry status symbols and he didn't want to hurt their feelings), he then began on his thank yous and goodbyes and finally, after taking a group photo, he bade them farewell. They wanted him to take Judah back to the land of milk and honey that (they supposed) Martin came from, but of course that was not possible.

Rather sadly Judah led Martin to the D'jema el F'na – the great souk and the purpose of his visit to Marrakech. On parting, Martin gave all the loose change he had on him to Judah for his kindness and trouble, but knew there was nothing he could really do to help: poverty on the scale in which it exists in the lost corners of this world is beyond individual action.

Judah accepted his gift, but as Martin turned to leave him Judah grabbed his sleeve; with a very worried look and pointing towards the souk heaving with assorted humanity in which Martin was about to be enveloped, Judah managed two words of English:

'Not good!'

…while clearly miming the certainty of pickpockets and the likelihood of getting his throat cut. Martin smiled what he hoped was a reassuring smile, squeezed the boy's shoulder and then, after several sincere seconds, Judah, the Jewish boy without hope and the big brown eyes, disappeared into the network of narrow alleys whence they'd just come. A friendship short and sweet. Martin remained standing thoughtfully in the shadows on the edge of the D'jema el F'na for some minutes. He reflected with humility on his grand life in Yorkshire. Was he as thankful for his good luck as he ought to be?

Martin's circle of concentration began to extend. He became aware of his surroundings. The famous market place on the edge of which Judah had left him took over. It was huge, it was very busy, it was the most exotic sight he'd ever seen. He was drawn into its blazing vortex; and now remembering David's advice: 'Don't forget – you just *must* see the snake charmer', he went in search of him.

Excited humanity was all around him now. There was shrieking and chattering and wailing and screeching – it was like Babel. There was selling and buying and pick-pocketing and bartering, everywhere there was money-making. The archetypal market place. Martin wandered around in this breathtaking environment; it was exerting a powerful fascination on him. Over there was someone swallowing scalding water for little coins thrown into his bucket; and there was another selling silks, and another rats (or were they puppies?) roasted on sticks. Here was a large circle of enthralled people, men, women and children, listening for the hundredth time to Bible stories told by a local prophet with the aid of a big coloured picture-book which he explained and embellished upon as he turned the pages.

Martin walked on. A delicious new experience was to be his good fortune: he always reckoned that life was for living, for discovering, for experiment; and the Barbary fig, eaten as you did right there on the street corner, was indeed a succulent experiment worth repeating… and repeating: you had to – at speed…! The Arab vendor was sitting cross-legged on the ground, a short sharp knife in his hand, a bucket of water beside him. Next to the bucket was a large pile of the green spiky fruit that looked a little like horse chestnuts. Martin paid his five francs and the Arab got to work: dip in the water; cut off the shell in a couple of deft strokes leaving the salmon-pink and juicy flesh of the fruit exposed; hand over to the client to eat.

Dip, cut off, and hand over to eat. Repeated a dozen times. You had to eat fast! The Barbary fig was delicious. Sweet and juicy it assuaged both thirst and hunger, but you had to gobble up with speed to keep up with your provider. It was a real conversation-stopper.

But the fun had to stop sometime and the next experience in the D'jema el F'na was not so good. No, not at all. His time was near now, but he still didn't know it. As he finished his fruity snack, he turned, and there, twenty yards away, he spotted it! The giant amphora, or water jar, exactly of the type that was one of the objects of his Moroccan holiday. Suddenly he realised the jar was the focus of an intent crowd and in the possession of a man with jet-black eyes of unfathomable profundity.

The jar was not for sale: it was very much in use. As he looked at the man who was squatting on a small Persian mat beside the jar, Martin smiled to himself:

'Looks just like Moriarty: ridiculous!'

...and as he approached, the hard thin line of the man's lips could be seen to curl upwards slightly and for an instant, then quickly disappeared. The man raised a pipe to his lips and gently played an enticing phrase. Instantly, the scaled head of a huge snake flashed out of the curvaceous neck of the water jar. The crowd gasped. Martin instinctively flinched. Twisting and turning, more and more of the snake's beautiful yet evil body appeared, searching, searching in all directions for something, something, something...

Would this monstrous reptile never end? It was now standing on its tail (which, of course, was hidden inside the four-foot-high jar) and projecting at least six feet into the air. Its head turned sharply this way and that, its tiny eyes bright and penetrating like the glint of blackest marquesite, its forked tongue shooting in and out in anticipation. Martin stood mesmerised by the sight: the snake charmer's pipe now raised the wordless song to a pitch of unbearable shrillness and hysterical urgency. Martin felt his heart pounding involuntarily. Eyes wide open, he was transfixed and could not believe what he saw and heard. The music climaxed and the snake spotted its quarry...

...then it spat with deadly accuracy. It spat its deadly line of poison, green as jealousy, like a dart. In one strike the evil snake achieved its target – the pupil of the right eye of Captain Martin Bigglesworth!

Martin yelled in excruciating pain and shock. Involuntarily his arm shot tensely upwards, his body convulsed violently and he collapsed, lifeless, to the ground.

The crowd closed in on his apparently lifeless body immediately, everyone screaming, shouting, clamouring, panicking. The snake hissed again, and with a collective gasp of horror and in fearful silence they backed away. The snake charmer, on whose lips the smile had returned and remained fixed (though no one had a thought to notice it), insinuated himself to M's lifeless side. Raising M's head in his hand he put his face close and observed. The snake charmer blew gently up M's nostrils. As Martin opened his eyes and semi-consciousness returned he became aware of the snake charmer's eyes: yes, he had seen them before and in the past couple of days, perhaps twice…

'That nice boy from Swansea told me you'd be here,' said the snake charmer in perfect English.

The eyes, the neatly trimmed black beard, the moustache and the cold smirk on his lips should have jolted Martin's recognition but he was semi-conscious, mentally confused, and he experienced only an escalating anxiety. His consciousness was going again. Going! Going! Gone!

When Martin came to, many hours later, the evening cool had already stolen into the huge square, and as he stiffly eased himself onto his elbow he realised the world had deserted him. Sitting on the dusty ground where he had fallen he saw he was now completely alone. He could hear the sounds of chanting in the distance. He examined himself but could find no hurt. Strange: but a relief. Beside him, however, was the amphora. M froze – would the snake spring out again? All was still. Then he noticed a label tied to one of the two finger-decorated handles. It read: *You came for this didn't you? Please accept it as a small souvenir – something to remember me by, something to add to your collection.* He turned the label over. *Something to make up for the pain you're going to suffer – I hope.*

M rose slowly to his feet; he felt fine, surprisingly. He brushed the dust off his clothes and for a brief moment or two was at a loss as to what to do. He was alive: that was good. Though he might not have been hurt, he was certainly badly shaken. He had no idea where he was or what he should do next; he felt very alone – he needed a friend.

As if in answer to his unspoken prayer a little lone figure appeared from the shadows a hundred yards away: it was Judah! The local bush telegraph had circulated the extraordinary event of the spitting snake and, when he heard the gossip, Judah guessed his new young English friend was certainly the one who had collapsed in agony and was probably dead. All the back-alley people were whispering in some fear how the snake charmer had frightened off the crowd with evil incantations and then, leaving with the snake entwined round his neck, had melted into thin air. It had so worried Judah that he'd come out at once looking for his friend.

Explanations between Martin and Judah were unnecessary; all was said that needed to be said in a glance:

'*Viens avec moi!*'

And taking the amphora thoughtfully from Martin's arms (Martin had checked to see the snake wasn't still inside!) Judah led our hero back to his family and the safe haven of the home of the poorest of the poor. Once there, the women enfolded him in their arms, literally and metaphorically, and plied him with mint tea and lots of sympathy; but Judah, having come to the rescue, left Martin in the care of his female relatives and scurried off back into the city without explanation.

The mint tea was calming and spiritually warming, and Martin, now centred and relaxed, was able to take stock of the situation. There were a host of questions regarding the incident of the snake charmer buzzing through his mind, of course, but time would surely supply answers. Martin first checked his money pouch, which he kept strapped round his waist under his shirt. Although he was doing his holiday on the cheap, youth hostelling, he nevertheless had a large emergency fund. This was certainly an emergency and, as his traveller's cheques and Barclaycard hadn't been stolen, the obvious first plan was a thoroughly spoiling "recovery night". A night on the Judah patch was on offer and very kind but not very comfortable… where to stay? There was no hesitation in Martin's mind: La Mamounia, arguably the best hotel in North Africa. That's what he'd do – spend one night of luxury in the hotel patronised at one time by none other than that Great

British War Leader, Sir Winston Churchill. He'd wait till Judah returned and get him to lead him there.

In spite of his night of luxury ahead, Martin couldn't forget the last sentence on the snake charmer's label… but as he was not the type to worry about things until they needed to be worried about he just finished his sweet tea quietly and wallowed in Judah's little citadel of love and generosity.

At that moment Judah reappeared with an older boy at his side.

'Ah Judah! *Ca va?*'

'I, ok – you, ok? Me, *tres* ok! Jesse, *mon frère*,' he announced proudly, introducing his elder brother.

'I get you nice bed?' said Jesse.

Now Jesse, it turned out, worked as a waiter at none other than La Mamounia! What a bit of luck! He could show Martin the way! So after another round of thank yous and goodbyes to Judah's family, he set off with the two boys to La Mamounia. At the entrance to the drive of the hotel Judah said his final farewell to Martin and turned back for home.

Little did Judah know that when he got home he'd find an envelope with a very generous present in it from Martin. To have put money directly into Judah's hand now that he was no longer just a hired urchin, Martin felt, would have cheapened their friendship – but certainly money was the most useful thing that lad could have wished for.

'*On y entre?*' enquired Jesse, and the two set off up La Mamounia's drive which wound lazily through heavily scented hoya and exuberant hibiscus, shady palm and giant cactus. The gardens at La Mamounia are famous the world over and Martin understood at once why the British Bulldog had chosen to immortalise them on canvas on one of his many stays there. A few hundred yards from the hotel's forecourt a little path to the left led off to the Staff Entrance, and it was down this path which Jesse now ran so as not to be late for the night shift.

The frightening and sinister incident in the D'jema el F'na was for the moment an almost faded memory in Martin's mind as he ascended the curving marble steps that beckoned him towards a Very Grand Entrance Indeed, dripping with bougainvillea. A servant in plum-coloured silk pantaloons obsequiously welcomed him into the cool air-conditioned foyer of the hotel, and soon he was relaxing in his luxury suite – a glacier-cool Gin and French in his hand of course!

'I've had a lucky escape,' thought Captain Martin Bigglesworth.

But he hadn't!

CHAPTER 6
THE KNIFE

ALTHOUGH MARTIN SLEPT like a log between silken sheets in the biggest bed he'd experienced since his own great Elizabethan four-poster in the Dales, he woke up unaccountably full of anxiety. Unaccountably? He accounted for his anxiety immediately. It was those eyes, black as coal, that kept worrying him – the eyes: where had he seen them before? As he lost consciousness for the second time yesterday in the D'jema el F'na their owner had been nose to nose with him. The profound power that glistened in those inky eyes of immaculate immobility welled up from the depths of a cruel confidence untold. Of course, oh reader, you had guessed way back in Chechauen to whom those eyes, that little beard and pencil moustache belonged; but then you were expecting Moriarty to turn up – our dear Captain was not: he was expecting to get away from it all.

Martin sat up in bed sharply on the realisation that it must indeed have been Moriarty who had somehow entered into his life – but worse, not just into his life: into his very body by means of the snake. The famous spitting snake of Morocco. Bile-green and deadly to behold – but (and he breathed a sigh of relief at this) not a poisonous snake at all. He inwardly thanked himself for his self-taught interest in exotic zoology (he had once written a paper on it) which had been born of his encounters with alien periphera. No, the Moroccan spitting snake, rare and evil-looking as it was, was definitely not poisonous: the spit produced immediate, excruciating but harmless pains, shock, temporary disorientation and mental confusion and finally unconsciousness, but no lasting effects.

Why then should Moriarty (for that was indeed who it was) want to introduce this non-toxic serum into his system? There seemed no rhyme – but he must have had a reason! Anyway he was not going to die of snake bite. He breathed a sigh of relief, dismissed reptilian reasonings from his mind, tugged the heavily tasselled bell-pull and ordered a large English breakfast – a great antidote to paranoia. Of course it might not have been Moriarty after all. M told himself he was being paranoid: no – it was definitely not Moriarty! Arabs always have dark eyes and hair and they frequently stare at you. He was putting two and two together and making five...

Until he remembered the label on his water jar. That was a bit inexplicable. A hoax perhaps from some idiot as he lay unconscious? And anyway what had Moriarty against him? Well, plenty really – they were opposites in every respect: where M was fair of skin and character, Moriarty was dark of both; where M was generous, Moriarty was mean; where M won, Moriarty lost. But surely that was all in the past?

He had left STOPIT: could he still be a threat to Moriarty? It was inexplicable. So he just lay back luxuriating on a mountain of down pillows, daydreaming about the second objective of his Moroccan holiday: the elusive Gnaoua belly dancers. At that moment a waiter entered with his breakfast on a large silver tray – and guess who it was? It was Jesse, Judah's elder brother, with the look of a film star.

'Your breakfast, Martin – and some extra *loukoumi* I've sneaked in for you under the table napkin,' he added with a twinkle in his eye. And sure enough, there it was: four cubes of pink and white Turkish Delight! Mmmm!

Now Jesse looked like a lad likely to know where belly dancers might be found. And sure enough, the information was immediately forthcoming. The waiter, whose eyes sparkled at the very mention of the girls, would not or could not give an address, but he did say positively there would be dancing, in the early hours that very night, and that he would lead M to whatever clandestine address at which they were to be found. M didn't need a second invitation – Gnaoua dancers are as hard to find as gold in a stream – but as it wouldn't have been quite *comme il faut* to be seen striding out of the front door of La Mamounia with a waiter at midnight, they made a private rendezvous under a particular large palm tree – one which M had already earmarked as a subject for his sketchpad later that day.

Jesse left, and Martin tucked into his thoroughly spoiling and rather piggy breakfast. Consisting of bacon, egg, tomatoes, mushroom, tea, croissants (Martin's only concession to foreign parts on this menu) and black-cherry jam (another little concession – well, Frank Cooper's Oxford marmalade was hard to come by in the foothills of the Blue Mountains that separated him so proximately from the Sahara Desert), this feast now filled not only his thoughts but his stomach.

Evening took a long time to come, as might have been expected; and M would have easily completed his watercolour of the palm tree if an Arab kid (they were everywhere) hadn't distracted him by flicking melon pips deliberately into his paint water to attract attention to himself. Eventually, the midnight assignation under the palm tree was achieved and M and the excited waiter set off for a destination unknown. This turned out to be a dark doorway at the end of a long alleyway in the oldest and darkest part of the *Ville Ancienne*. M crossed his fingers that his guide wouldn't do a disappearing trick halfway through the night, because he would have been totally and utterly lost; it could have been dangerous too as he would have been an easily spotted quarry alone in the dark alleyway. A prime target for the mugger's knife. M obliterated this negative thinking from his mind; anyway, the beat of the drums and the rustle of bejewelled fringes he could hear ahead were making his heart beat faster in anticipation.

'Down here.' Jesse led him down precipitous stone steps to a subterranean cavern. Out of the shadows a girl appeared wearing but a jewel in her belly button and a skimpy fringe of beads and tassels. The jewel was extravagant, it is true, but the fringes were definitely economic.

Then other girls appeared from nowhere and the gyrations began. Martin could not take his eyes off the flashing emeralds and rubies and sapphires. These undulating pulsating bellies were not the "poetry in motion" upmarket travel writers pretend – they were downright erotic and M almost felt the urge to participate. The muscles in his own stomach began to quiver in sympathy. His stomach positively rippled – so much so that he had to employ considerable mental bromide to stop the contractions. When he realised he was becoming more interested in his own unjewelled anatomy than the beautiful girls but inches away from him, he said to himself: 'Something must be wrong here.' And it was.

It was at this point that M began to feel most strange. Not only were his stomach muscles moving involuntarily, but a pain deep inside him was growing: a pain the like of which he had never before experienced. It was not – to start with – exactly a sharp pain but it brought with it a strange feeling of fear. The fear quickly developed into panic: he felt he was swelling up inside; the mildish pain became acute agony. Real pain. He wondered if he could tolerate it any longer. That was all he remembered.

Hours later he opened his eyes.

'How do you feel now?' A well-modulated voice close to his ear awakened our hero, who was surprised to find that he was back in his hotel suite at La Mamounia.

'Fine,' said M, 'but how did I get here?'

'A waiter from La Mamounia carried you back. By chance I'm on a surgical conference here with my wife. Apparently last night when you were watching belly dancers you collapsed: you appear to be suffering from an acute colic attack,' said the surgeon – for it was to a surgeon indeed that the well-modulated voice turned out to belong. 'It's evidently over now, but you could have another one at any time. Without access to proper equipment I can't tell you any more, and I'm afraid the hospitals here aren't really up to either a full diagnosis or the cure!'

'What is the likely diagnosis, doctor?'

'Gallstones.'

'And what is the cure, doctor?' asked Martin a little anxiously.

'The knife,' was the terse reply. 'Of course it is only my hunch, based on some thirty years' experience; I would want to have you scanned and other tests performed before I confirmed this advice. But probably you're going to need a cholecystectomy within the next six weeks.'

'A what?'

'You're going to need your gall bladder removed. You've probably developed a gallstone or stones which have moved and blocked up the duct that releases your bile. You're obstructed, hence the strange feeling and fearful pain you experienced.'

'Is it a big operation?' Martin was not a coward, but anyone listening would be forgiven if they thought they heard a little tremor in his voice.

'It's a major operation'.

'I can put up with the periodic pain – so what if I just leave it?'

'It'll kill you.'

Martin was silent for a moment. Then: 'What should I do?'

'Go back to England as soon as the present colic attack has settled. The quality of the surgery and nursing is better in Britain than anywhere in the world, even if the facilities are often Victorian, the slender staff exhausted, the food appalling, and the whole chaos is in thrall to Political Correctness and politically motivated Administrators. Get a second opinion if you want.'

When the surgeon had gone, Martin immediately reached for the phone and rang his father, an internationally famous surgeon and an expert in this field himself.

'Well, it's up to you,' his father said a moment or two later, 'but it certainly does sound like an acute colic attack. I wonder what brought it on so suddenly though.' He was puzzled. 'Very strange – stones like that always take years to develop... you haven't ever had any symptoms have you?'

'No.' M's mind was racing; was there a connection, he wondered, between the snake spit and the sudden growth of a stone within him? If that snake charmer really had been Moriarty after all then this was well within the realms of possibility. But why would anyone want to kill him – now a veteran of twenty-five – and in such an elaborate way?

'Sounds like too much belly dancing and snakey business,' his father suggested a little unsympathetically.

M's mind was still occupied with his Moriarty hypothesis.

'Are you there? Are you there?' his father was asking. 'What's the matter with you? Why don't you answer?'

M didn't disclose his fantasmagorical solution in case his father thought he'd lost his marbles; instead he asked:

'Where should I go to have it removed? Who should I get to do it?'

'You'll need to have tests first to double-check. Edinburgh's good. The Royal Infirmary: they still believe in discipline and hygiene in Scotland. I'll write a note to the top man.'

M's holiday in Morocco was well and truly over, and twenty-four hours later he was in Scotland – in a hospital bed.

CHAPTER 7
ROYAL INFIRMARY, SCOTLAND

THE INFIRMARY CONFIRMED the presence of one enormous gallstone and recommended immediate surgery. There was no time to think about it, and before M knew where he was he was being prepared for the operation to remove it.

'Lucky for you it didn't blow up in the middle of the desert,' said a kindly Sister from the Highlands. 'It could have killed you.' She nearly added 'It still might' but thought better of it as the expression on M's face clearly indicated he didn't need reminding: he know the score. 'Drink this: they'll be coming to take you down to the theatre in a moment,' she said. 'Don't worry – you'll be back here before you can say "haggis" and it'll all be over.' Then she left.

'All be over… it might well be…' but M was helpless and could do nothing but let fate take its course.

Moments later a theatre porter arrived and helped him onto a trolley. It turned out he was a recent drama student waiting for his big break; little did he know he'd landed himself in the front line of Moriarty's next attack.

'I'm Simon,' he said.

He could have been the Sultan of Morocco as far as M was concerned as he was already feeling woozy from the pre-op draught the Sister had given him. M was now being wheeled briskly to the operating theatre, and Simon was burbling on about some audition he was up for when he was suddenly interrupted by another voice and a sharp exchange ensued behind his head; but the new voice seemed vaguely familiar. The second voice said in a cool and authoritative tone:

'Let me take him into the theatre – then I can pick up any little stones that fall out onto the floor, you know, when they open him up.'

'No, I'm sorry,' said the astute Simon, who sensed something was wrong. 'I'm not allowed to hand over my patient to anyone because...' But he never finished his sentence.

'Look at me,' whined the second porter. 'In – to – my – eyes. Now hand over this patient.'

'If you say so, sir,' said Simon in a dreamy way, and walked off like a zombie. The new porter moved round the trolley and smiled at Martin. It was the smile of the snake charmer.

'I want you to suffer,' he said.

M was horrified and helpless and unable to prevent the inevitable, and before he could utter a sound the anaesthetist had sent him swiftly into oblivion with a little prick in his thumb.

Back in the ward, tubed in all directions, M was at last out of intensive care. They'd had a tricky time with him as he'd started shouting for a meringue which caused considerable frivolity in the resuscitation ward until his shouts gave way to such yells of agony that they'd had to up his morphine injection to a dangerous level. The formidable but highly efficient and deeply caring Sister was finally organising him. She held up a pound jam-jar.

'This is your gallstone.' Inside the jar, stinking with formaldehyde, was a stone an inch long – and to Martin's amazement it was an exact miniature of a shape he knew only too well: it was the amphora-shaped water jar from the D'jema el F'na!

'That's incredible – it's exactly the same shape as...' and M wisely checked himself from linking the gallstone with the amphora in Marrakech, the spitting snake and Moriarty because he was afraid the Sister would think he'd gone clinically mad and might have felt inclined to add to his discomfort by putting him in a straitjacket; so he added simply:

'May I keep it? I'll put it with my collection of Phoenician and Greco-Roman tear vases – no one will ever know the difference and I'll have fun teasing the experts!'

'I'll put it in your bedside cupboard here; now you rest and get a bit of sleep.'

M slipped back almost instantly into unconsciousness. The Sister left him in his private room alone. A little later the door was opened very slowly and silently by a plastic-gloved hand, the hand of the second porter – though porter he was not – and he quickly crossed the room to M's bedside cupboard.

In an instant the jar containing his amphora-shaped gallstone was in his hand. The intruder turned and was already advancing towards the door when the Sister appeared on the threshold – she had left her scissors behind...

'Who are you? I've never seen you before. What have you got there? Give that to me.'

'That's all right, Sister,' purred the "porter" with the dark eyes and the neatly trimmed black beard and moustache. 'I'm from the research department. We need to make some tests on this most unusual stone. Allow me to pass please.'

'No.' The Sister barred the door and the "porter" (which of course he wasn't) then tried his hypnotism trick on her.

'That won't work on me,' said the determined Sister. 'I'm not susceptible! I want your credentials immediately, or that jar.' At this the porter attempted to push her aside – she was only a woman after all. What he hadn't taken into account was that she was a black belt in Aikido. In a flash she had the bottle and the "porter" was biting the dust halfway up the corridor. It was clear her Thursday afternoon lessons had paid off. The sister called for help; it looked as if the "porter", who'd scrambled to his feet and was legging it, would be cornered because by a bit of good luck two housemen appeared at the end of each corridor. However, Moriarty (for yes, it was indeed he, in yet another disguise) hesitating but a moment, leapt through a first-floor window and made his getaway across The Meadows, and was lost in the darkness of a moonless Edinburgh night.

Much later, in the early hours of the morning, the Sister was sitting on the end of M's bed (he'd regained consciousness fully now) and she told him of the incident which to her was inexplicable. To M, however, the pieces of the jigsaw were coming together, but he couldn't say what he thought; well – what he knew. Planet Earth was undoubtedly under threat again, and the gallstone had to be of some prime significance, but as yet he knew not what.

Captain Martin Bigglesworth, recently of STOPIT, realised that quite unwittingly he was in the thick of a new and clearly mortal adventure whether he liked it or not.

He liked it!

CHAPTER 8
THE AMPHORA CALCULOSA

CAPTAIN MARTIN BIGGLESWORTH had had a narrow escape, but he was back home now in the Yorkshire Dales and making a quick recovery: he'd been in tip top condition (as always) before his operation. He was determined now to get fit again as quickly as possible.

He knew that getting over any illness was a matter of willpower and lay largely in the mind. He also knew that somewhere in some dark and sinister corner Moriarty would have been festering for the past two weeks while he had been in hospital, plotting his next strike to get his hands on Martin's gallstone. He had known that nothing further could happen while it was safely in his keeping and he was in the security of the hospital. Now he was home, however, anything could happen – and probably would.

He didn't have long to wait. As he scanned the *Darlington Northern Echo* and caught up with the local news, Douggie, another of his very loyal stable lads, emerged with several letters.

'For you, Martin; anything else you want?'

'Not a thing thanks – unless you've got a winner for me.'

'The talk is Jamie's got a good chance in the two thirty at Cheltenham.' Martin loved a tip and a flutter, but he was no gambler. His interest in horse racing was aesthetic and social – only the bookies and trainers made money. Horse-racing to Martin was simply great fun, and his Colours – Purple and Yellow stripes with a Purple cap with Yellow Spots – hang behind the door of his flat in London to this day.

Back to the day's mail. Martin loved to prolong the moment when he actually opened the envelopes and would play a guessing game with himself as to what they contained. Then he'd arrange them in reverse order of interest and open them up.

There was one from Wetherby's – a racing bill; council tax; income tax; junk mail… (he hated junk mail). The writing on the next one looked young and the doodles on the envelope gave its authorship away. Our soldier hero received a constant stream of letters from military enthusiasts, and with a delighted 'Ah!' Martin broke his rules of letter-opening and opened this one straight away. 'Thought so – how very kind,' he mumbled under his breath. These letters always contained the nicest compliments and usually a request for a signed photograph. Now a blue envelope was in his hands – a dye-stamped crest in even deeper blue on the flap of the envelope of very heavily laid paper indicated an aristocratic source. And finally – now what was this? A North London postmark? Could it be? Quickly he slipped his silver art-nouveau paper-knife into the envelope to discover it was from… 'The Bum!' It was indeed from General Augustus, his old military commander; and, would you believe it, he'd been invited to a shooting party at Melmerby with an ex-army friend and distant cousin of Martin's mother. This cousin, Bob, had a splendid grouse moor comprising Penn Hill, the dominating feature in this part of the Pennines. The hill can be seen in the background of a prize-winning portrait of Martin by Christopher Thompson. The shoot was not four miles from Martin's house and in the letter the General proposed to call on him first. Somehow the letter, although first class, had got well delayed in the post (how unusual!) and the General was due up in Yorkshire the very next day. Martin reached for his phone at once and seconds later the old friends were making last-minute arrangements.

'See you tomorrow for lunch, General. Excellent!' And then Martin added with a telephonic twinkle: 'I picked up something most interesting in Morocco to add to my collection – a rare, nay unique, object. I'll show it to you tomorrow… bye.'

The Bum sounded in top form and he was clearly anticipating excellent hospitality for his weekend's shooting party as his hostess Gillie, a Scot, was known throughout Yorkshire for her lavish table and her husband – who owned most of Coverdale – for his Chateau Mouton Rothschild '45. The General had therefore taken the prudent precaution of not drinking and driving and had enlisted the services of none other than Warrant Officer Bloggs to be his chauffeur for the weekend. Smudge too! Martin couldn't believe it: in twenty-four hours he'd be seeing once again his two dear comrades-in-arms. His pleasure would have been complete if Dizzy and Sniffles had been coming as well.

'What can I give them to eat?' mused Martin. He loved entertaining and although he would never lay claim to be a comprehensive chef, he was known to have cooked some very much above-average meals.

'Something substantial for the main course,' he thought – 'they'll have driven two hundred and fifty miles and they are both big eaters!' What could be better than local lamb? Freshly slaughtered and butchered in Middleham by Harry Pickersgill, with mint sauce (mint from Martin's herb garden) and crabapple jelly (home-made by Martin from fruit from his prolific John Downey tree). Young runner beans and new potatoes. Simple and good. Potted shrimps encouraged by a glass of Tio Pepe to start with. What about a pudding? Port wine jelly perhaps. (That took a pint of port to make and, though they tasted good, his jellies usually collapsed. Not that The Bum would mind as the contents would be very much up his street!) Or Yorkshire lemon pudding? Yes, this simple seventeenth-century Yorkshire recipe was light and tangy and would be nice after the lamb. No, both! Finally, Wensleydale cheese and russets would complete the meal. A Gin and French when they arrived with salted almonds, which Martin would roast himself, would get them in a good mood. He had a very good, but not at all expensive, red Chilean Rioja for the lamb. A glass of pudding wine to be followed by Old Bushmill's Irish whiskey. The General of course would not actually be firing a shot till the following day, so the rest of the party would not be put at risk by Martin's hospitality. Smudge could have orange juice – he was driving!

Ironic, he mused to himself as he wrote "Hildon Water" on the shopping list, that while he drank the clear sweet spring water in primitive Morocco, no one now drank the tap water in North Yorkshire! While the chairman and directors of the privatised water companies had all become millionaires, ordinary Yorkshire folk could no longer enjoy God's wine. The bonuses alone some of the fat-cat chief execs and bankers received annually could give a higher education to dozens of local students so unfairly denied a chance in life. Martin fumed to himself: can a country call itself civilised or even basically fair when the best of education, health care and a decent safe home to live in are available only if you are rich enough to afford it? Apart from the immorality, how foolish of a state to surpress all this potential future talent.

Martin stopped himself getting too worked up about the unfairness of British society as he had a busy time organising things, and before you could say 'Whippet One' the clanging of the heavy and ancient bronze bell in the hall the next day announced the arrival of his friends. To cut a dash Bloggs had skidded the General's big Citroen by the front door and removed the top layer of gravel from the drive. They greeted each other like long-lost friends, however, and Smudge was immediately given a yard-brush to obliterate the aforementioned skid-marks.

On entering the house, Smudge then cracked his head on a low beam in a small downstairs closet and followed it up by cracking an appalling joke. This cracked the stable lads up who happened to be listening, but left the General with a blank expression on his face and convinced Martin nothing had changed.

'Come and have a drink,' said Martin, and the General and Bloggs followed their host into his thoroughly baronial library. They took in with amazement the gallery extending round two complete walls of the former chapel, and Martin did his usual trick of waiting till they'd seen it all before dramatically opening the panelling at one end of the room to disclose a secret bedroom.

The Captain and the General got stuck into the gin while Bloggs started on his first of many orange juices. (Martin had thoughtfully already had a packet of Imodium placed beside Smudge's bed with a carafe of water.)

'I believe you told General Hycock-Bottomley you'd got a souvenir in Morocco you wanted to show us, Captain,' hazarded the Warrant Officer.

'Well, hardly a souvenir – a most rare pre-Delphinian amphora-shaped tear vase. It's in the cabinet with my other Greco-Roman pieces.' They crossed the room and looked into a glass cabinet full of ancient relics.

'It's a miniature version of a water or wine jar,' the General pronounced with the confidence of a Field Marshal. 'Very subtle colouring: definitely a find, Martin. What period would you say it was?'

'Oh, 300 BC,' lied Martin.

'You know Martin, your Greco-Roman artefact looks uncannily like that – probably mythical – Amphora Calculosa the Professor's always going on about: the Excalibur of the Cosmos, the Guardians Of Time's "Holy Grail". He's always wanted to discover how to make one.'

At that second, as sometimes happens in life, a chance flippancy from one person revealed a blinding truth to another. In a flash M made the vital link between his gallstone and the Amphora Calculosa: they were one and the same! Moriarty had done it!

Martin retired into deep thought; the implications were cataclysmic. Bloggs looked lost.

'Lost, Bloggs?'

'Yes, General.'

'Well Bloggs – and you won't know this, Martin – STOPIT got wind of close-to-final experiments Moriarty was making to find a way of producing an Amphora Calculosa synthetically. If he succeeded he would have it in his power to make the ultimate cosmic handgun. By an extraordinary coincidence we in STOPIT had a flash report from one of our double-agents we were using in Morocco, only the day you left for your holiday Martin, to say that Moriarty appeared to be on the point of realising his dark dream. He was, not to put too fine a point on it, within an ace of making his fatal discovery.'

'Fatal?' queried Bloggs. 'Well, that's great – he'll probably kill himself.'

'Don't be silly Bloggs: not fatal to him, but when mass-produced it will be capable of exterminating every human being on the planet. The Amphora Calculosa – stone-like in consistency and in the shape of an ancient Roman wine- or water-carrying amphora – is the final component in Moriarty's hideous weapon of mass human elimination, the mere handgun-sized MMG…'

'MMG?' Bloggs was riveted by the story of undercover double espionage the General was about to reveal.

'MMG stands for Matter Mincing Gun.'

'With a scoop of mashed potato on your head, Bloggs, it could reduce you to a cottage pie,' quipped Martin. As M hoped, Smudge and The Bum found the image funny, and were diverted from the subject and the awful truth that the object in M's cabinet of antiquities was not his gallstone at all: it was the actual Amphora Calculosa of fantasy realised – and he who held it would rule the Universe. Now Martin knew why Moriarty was so anxious to get his hands on his handiwork. His experiments had succeeded – and in Martin's gallbladder!

A blackly humorous pun came to Martin's mind: *He nearly killed two birds with one stone.* But Martin was still very much alive, and he had possession of the Amphora Calculosa; the cards were all in his hands. There was a glimmer of hope in the situation after all. However, if Moriarty were ever to get hold of the "gallstone" (and M knew he'd stop at nothing to try), he could reduce a whole nation of Goliaths into a hill of ants in the blink of an eye.

The remarkable and very lucky thing was that the General and Bloggs still believed M's gallstone was a priceless treasure from the antique world. Well, academia to them would probably have sounded like a mental illness had they stumbled on the word!

'Very shapely I'd call it, sir,' leered Bloggs. 'Many a good woman would envy a figure like that Amphora thingy' – and at the thought the General went all misty-eyed. A vision of Ada had clearly arisen in his mind's eye – but silently Martin smiled wickedly wondering whether it was the shape that reminded him of her, or its blotchy, rough and pock-marked surface.

Said Martin: 'Did your double-agent have a Welsh accent, General?'

'He did! How on earth did you know?'

'I didn't: just my offbeat sense of humour.' To M another piece of the jigsaw had fallen into place: David from Swansea was a double-agent!

At this point, Martin would have loved to have spilled the beans and told them it was actually not a gallstone at all and that it had been planted by Moriarty in the guise of the snake charmer, using a rare Moroccan spitting snake to induce its poisonous serum into his bile duct through his right eye. He would have loved to have shared with them his Earth-shaking knowledge, but he didn't dare to – yet. With his recent reputation for loss of critical judgement they'd probably regard him as even softer in the head than before, and would (regretfully) confirm in their minds that STOPIT's Top Brass decision to retire him from the team had been the correct one. Poor Martin – he would always cherish the hope of a recall to arms, even if the chance was nil, but he needed yet more evidence that it was indeed Moriarty (though he had no doubts himself) before he dared broach the subject with his friends. Moriarty had to reveal his identity openly in front of STOPIT first. So he just said:

'Sorry both of you – just jesting – had you for a couple of minutes – it was my gallstone!' and before they could suffer embarrassment he changed the subject. 'Come and have lunch'. The lunch went with a swing; Smudge made up on food what he had lost in alcohol and after a good belch at the end of the meal declared he was full. 'I should jolly well hope so!' said Martin with a smile. 'You ate eleven potatoes!'

'Sir...' said Bloggs suddenly, 'I've had a great idea!' The General and the Captain groaned inwardly and their eyes met without giving anything away.

'Oh yes,' said the General defensively.

'Really,' said the Captain, and added with the minimum of enthusiasm, 'Do tell us'.

'That amphibious Roman pot…'

'You mean the pre-Delphinian amphora-shaped Roman tear vase?' corrected the Captain helpfully.

'Yes sir – that's the thing. Why don't we play your gallstone gag you just played on us, on The Brain? He always thinks he knows everything about the ancient world… and that Van Gogh yellow banger of his – he loves old crocks.'

'So does the General,' murmured Martin *sotto voce* to Smudge; 'look at Ada!' They giggled together like a couple of schoolboys.

'Frankly,' added Smudge, 'I don't think he knows the difference between a Greek Myth and a Roman Missus!' and then laughed loudly at his own appalling witticism.

'Not a good idea,' warned Martin, 'The Brain won't see the joke.'

'I think it's a great idea,' insisted Bloggs – where's your sense of humour sir?'

'On your heads be it!'

A polaroid camera was produced, the gallstone was photographed surrounded by artefacts of genuine antiquity, and they faxed off the photographs with a suitable accompanying message. General Augustus then decided he'd like to have a long constitutional with Martin to walk off their lunch and Bloggs was left (at his own request) to hold the fort. Whether WO Bloggs was being tactful in giving the Captain and his former commanding officer time to be on their own to discuss – as he put it – 'officers' matters', or whether it was that after his long drive and eleven spuds he wanted a snooze, we shall never know. The General and the Captain did indeed stride off for a brisk and beautiful walk, but Bloggs was not to be so lucky in getting forty winks. He was now to have an adventure all of his own…

He waved the two officers off and before snoozing remembered a joke he thought would go down well with the stable lads: Jock and Julien were the unlucky victims he collared, but his joke failed to raise the faintest of smiles even from Julien, a nice French lad who'd normally laugh at anything to hide the fact that he understood nearly nothing. Not a snigger. It was something about a man with a sore throat who entered the wrong door of a country surgery and instead of consulting the GP for some cough linctus, had seen the vet by mistake who, having asked him what the matter was and been told 'I'm a little hoarse,' had promptly had the man tranquillised, sectioned and sent to the local loony-bin. Bloggs had laughed till the tears flowed down his rough and ruddy cheeks, so he hadn't noticed the fact that the two lads hadn't laughed at all. In fact he found it so funny he thought he'd try it on the General and the Captain when they returned. In the event he didn't get an opportunity for joke-telling or for snoozing, as Fate intervened...

Scarcely had the joke flopped, and the lads left to swim in the river, than an immaculate black Bentley S1 Continental purred up the drive. The joke instantly forgotten, Bloggs drooled, and he waited at the door as its owner/driver (an immaculately dressed man in a black suit, with a neat well-trimmed black beard and moustache, and whose eyes were concealed behind impenetrably dark glasses) pulled up, and approached him.

'Is zees Captain Martin Bigglesvorth's residence?' the Bentley driver enquired with a heavy German accent.

'Yes sir – but the Captain's just gone out.'

'May I come in and vait for him?'

'He'll probably be a couple of hours – or more.'

'I don't mind how long I vait – I've all zee time in zee vorld. And zee next...' he added mysteriously: a point not lost on the Warrant Officer. However, any doubts Bloggs might have had about the visitor, or that little voice in the back of his mind which told him to be careful, he suppressed. Why? It was simple: Bloggs's gut feeling for second-hand car salesmanship had been well activated by that gleaming machine in the background, and all doubts were obliterated. He must be all right with a car like that, thought the easily impressed WO.

'Please come in, sir.'

The dark and elegant visitor held out a black-gloved hand and offered Bloggs his card. Bloggs, who could read of course, read it. It read:

WOLFGANG von MYCROFT-HOLMES
Antiquities
221B Baker Street, London
and 13 Potsdamer Platz, Berlin

'Will you have a seat?' offered Bloggs, politely indicating an uncomfortable antique wooden hall-chair – one of a small collection Martin was making.

'*Danke.*'

Silence.

'Nice day?' suggested Bloggs helpfully.

'*Was sagen zee?*'

'Zee? Oh! You'd like a cup of *tea*? I'll get you one.'

Bloggs came back with two cups and, uninvited, joined the rich foreigner for a chat which regrettably took a dangerous turn. It turned out that the German antique-dealer had heard of Martin's collection of Greco-Roman and Phoenician tear vases from one Henry Archibald Thomas Etherington...

'An MP, you know,' said von Mycroft-Holmes, shrewdly realising that Bloggs would be impressed. 'I expect you've heard of him: a great art collector.'

'Oh yes of course,' said Bloggs who hadn't, but wanted to show he was up there with the cognoscenti.

'Who in zee art vorld hasn't heard of him?' Bloggs was certainly one, but he didn't let on.

The German explained that, as he was in the area at a private viewing of a catalogue sale at Tennant's of Leyburn, the famous auctioneers, he thought he'd drop in on Captain Bigglesworth and discuss the possibility of including some of the Captain's artefacts in an international exhibition he was organising in Paris shortly. Bloggs responded that of course he couldn't be sure if the Captain would be interested, but he might well be.

'A chocolate biscuit?' invited Bloggs to keep the conversation going.

'*Nein.*'

'That's a bit greedy isn't it?' Bloggs howled at his own joke. '*Nein* – nine chocolate biscuits – get it? Get it?' The German said nothing, but it was poor Bloggs who got it later.

This time he noticed the rich and important von Mycroft-Holmes wasn't laughing and, as Bloggs was basking in his illustrious company and wanted to continue rubbing shoulders with him, he desperately wracked his brain for another witticism. Von Mycroft-Holmes' visiting card which was in his hand gave him the idea:

'I see you're from the Black Forest, mein Herr.' (He thought his knowledge of German titles would impress.)

'*Ja.*'

'Nice gateau down there,' trumped Bloggs and laughed quite loudly. But the antique dealer's scornful look was not lost on him and he fell silent while the German simply turned his attention to a copy of *The Field* which was at hand.

It was some hours later when Bloggs had his "eureka moment". As the sun was setting, and the two officers had still not returned from their constitutional walk, Bloggs chuckled to himself. 'I'll swing the gallstone gag on this foreigner: I'll make him feel small,' thought Bloggs, who'd been shrunk inwardly and wanted to reinflate himself.

'Would you like to see the Captain's latest acquisition?' he ventured. It worked better than he could possibly have dreamed. The German leapt to his feet.

'Show it to me at once. *Snell! Snell! Snell! Du dummer Engelsman!*'

Swedish? thought Bloggs, who spotted a clue – to what he knew not.

'I have a Svedish lady-friend: Lena is very friendly to me,' snapped Moriarty, who'd read Bloggs' mind. '*Du dummer Engelsman!*'

Bloggs couldn't be sure if he'd been paid a compliment or not, but he didn't care; he'd obviously excited the visitor which was his intention.

'Please follow me.' Bloggs led the dark visitor to the cabinet where Martin's gallstone had pride of place.

'There – an Ambitious Delphinium which belonged to a Tearful Roman. Mint condition,' added Smudge, the instinctive salesman. 'Circa 500 BBC,' he concluded, crossing his fingers that he wouldn't be asked to justify his claim.

'I know you idiot – I am zee expert in zees field!' Bloggs didn't mind the insult: he'd won over the antique dealer game, set and match. He couldn't believe his luck when the dealer went on:

'I'll give you five hundred pounds for eet!'

'Double it,' said the emboldened Warrant Officer. 'The Captain wouldn't take a penny less than a thousand.' To his amazement, without a word, the stranger produced one thousand pounds in new notes.

'Give eet to me at vonce, I must be off...'

'But I thought you wanted to see...'

'I can't vait forever.' And before Bloggs could collect his wits, Wolfgang von Mycroft-Holmes' number plate was only just readable, as the black Bentley sped off down the drive. Bloggs did read it, however, and it gave him just a moment's heart tremor. It was a personalised plate comprising three letters and the number 1, which was clearly intended to be read as the letter I. It read – EVIL!

'Evil! Oh Lord!' thought Bloggs. 'Could it have been...'

But Martin and General Augustus returned at that very moment and Bloggs never actually heard the dreadful penny drop in what passed for his brain.

'Been entertaining the plutocracy in my absence, Smudge?' quipped Martin who'd almost been driven off his own drive into the rhododendrons that lined it by the accelerating limousine.

'Well, yes, sir.' Bloggs hadn't a clue what the plutocracy might be, but he was intelligent enough to assume that the Captain meant the owner of the black Bentley.

'As a matter of fact Captain, I've done a bit of a deal for you. You'll be pleased,' Bloggs added, assuming Martin would be delighted. Clasping the thousand pounds in his left hand, he put both hands behind his back.

'Which hand will you have?'

'Which hand? What are you talking about?'

'Which hand, Captain? Choose!' Bloggs was grinning so broadly even the General looked suspicious.

'Right,' said Martin.

'Left – but you can have it anyway.' Bloggs offered him the money. 'I got rid of that old gallstone of yours.'

'What!'

'I sold it to that man who's just left in the S1 for a thousand pounds – here it is.'

'Bother.'

'I beg your pardon Captain? Will you take the money, sir?'

As he took the thousand pounds Bloggs proffered, Martin had a distinctly faraway look: he was thinking fast. The dark evil guest was Moriarty, and this gallstone – which he knew would soon activate the only MMG in the Cosmos – was now in Moriarty's hands; and Moriarty had gone, he knew not where. Involuntarily he screwed the thousand pounds into a ball and in absent-minded frustration threw the notes into the blazing fire. The General gasped with horror while Bloggs dived for the money and burnt his fingers on the grate.

'It's got to be Moriarty,' Martin thought to himself. 'It's got to be.' But out loud he said: 'I'm going out for a bit; the run of the house is yours, but just don't sell anything else while I'm gone, right? Dinner is at eight thirty. I'll see you in the library at eight fifteen.' And with that he left the room.

'He never said thank you,' murmured Bloggs.

'I don't think he was very pleased,' observed the General. And with that the conversation ceased.

Martin had been very tempted to enlighten his friends at this point as to the identity of the Bentley driver, but so keen was he to solve the problem on his own, and prove to his former STOPIT colleagues that he was indeed fit again now, that he decided to withhold his information just a little longer.

At dinner that evening no more was said about the matter, and Martin with characteristic generosity entertained his friends to the best champagne from his cellar; and, as Bloggs was now off duty so far as driving was concerned, he was allowed to participate in the bubbly. So much did he enjoy his Captain's hospitality, in fact, that later he had to be escorted to bed by two senior officers of the British Army.

CHAPTER 9
BREAD SOLDIERS

ONLY MARTIN AND the stable lads saw dawn break over Coverdale the next morning. The rosy fingers of the sun caressed this beautiful and remote corner of North Yorkshire, at first creating and then (as the dew dried off, and the air above and the earth below more nearly equalled each other's temperature) dispelling a gossamer mist, to reveal an absolutely clear blue sky. Later the morning contours would give way to the direct overhead light and heat of the midday sun, but now the sun was gentle, and low on the horizon, and at the crest of the gallops a string of racehorses stood out in silhouette as they set out on their morning exercise.

General Augustus and WO Bloggs, who'd imbibed well the night before, overslept and (if the truth were told, which it now has been) missed the magnificence of early morning on the Middleham Gallops. When they descended eventually to the breakfast room, they found their host had already nearly finished and was treating his cat, Charles Tyrone Smith, to some ends of smoked salmon to which he was very partial.

'Morning both,' said Martin. 'Did you sleep well?'

'Like a log,' said Bloggs quietly (he had a dreadful hangover).

An apt description, thought M. 'Have some toast.'

'Thank you,' whispered the fragile Bloggs, and as he aimed for the bread he bumped into the table unsteadily and sent a pound of farmhouse butter flying onto the flagstone floor.

'Like a log,' echoed the General – who was a great echoer of other people's *bon mots* – 'like a log.'

'Help yourselves,' offered their generous host. No sooner were the two hung-over guests settled at the table confronting their boiled eggs than the phone rang.

'It's for you,' declared Martin handing the receiver across the table to the General. 'It's the Prof and he doesn't sound very pleased; I believe he's received your message.' The General took the phone (after a split-second decision whether to do so or not, it must be noted) and, with an ultimate decisiveness that indicated his courage, in a clear, deep and brave voice that left the listener in no doubt as to his suitability for command of STOPIT, he said:

'Good morning, Professor – Hycock-Bottomley here.'

'You're an idiot,' said the voice on the phone, 'a first-class idiot.'

'Quite so, Professor,' concurred the affronted General, inwardly ruffled though he didn't show it lest the junior officers at the breakfast table should detect his telephonic carpeting. (Actually, they had heard clearly as the volume was at maximum and the Professor's voice could be heard halfway up the Dale.)

'What are you?' the Professor persisted.

'An idiot, Professor – a first-class idiot.' Martin and Smudge caught each other's glance and choked with laughter; the General reddened. Considering the lifetime of good living that showed on his nose and cheeks, and with the rays of rosy morning sunlight that were streaming through the mullioned windows, you can imagine, oh reader, that the General's already glowing visage was now an enticing shade of magenta.

'I've just received your fax: do you not recognise an Amphora Calculosa when you see one?'

'Amphora Calculosa?' repeated the poor General, stunned. 'It was an Amphora Calculosa? We thought it was just Captain Bigglesworth's gallstone.'

A look of total understanding passed over the General's face. He now understood why the snake had spat in Martin's eye. Moriarty had used him as a host to a deadly bacterium which clearly could not fulfil its growth cycle except in the human bile duct. A disgusting and frightening thought: his unfortunate 2-I/C had been the surrogate father to an alien!

The General shuddered. To Bloggs (who, as usual, was in the dark), he whispered only the essential facts: 'The Amphora Calculosa now makes Moriarty with his MMG invincible.'

Now, for those of you who are interested in the technicalities of death, the MMG or Matter Mincing Gun is no longer a theory or a myth or a Holy Grail, but a hideous reality and it works like this: the rays produced by means of the chemico-molecular activity of the Amphora Calculosa cause a hundred per cent H_2O deficiency in human matter, which – accompanied by a symbiotic degradation of the residual desiccated fibres – reduces the target to a mere 0.035 per cent of its original size. That is how in an encounter that occurred some years later (when the Falkland Islands were attacked by a South American Dictator and STOPIT came to the rescue in what became known as "The Great Tea Bag Mystery") a certain female Prime Minister of Great Britain was reduced to the size of a teabag and came to be lost forever in an old teapot. With the Amphora Calculosa in his possession Moriarty was once again a vile and fearful threat to all good men, women and children of planet Earth. The scenario was doom-laden. No wonder the Professor was in a foul mood.

'You should have recognised it,' repeated the Professor. 'Lucky Moriarty isn't about: if he'd got his hands on it your little world would really be in trouble'.

'I'm sorry, Prof,' muttered the gutted General lamely.

'Well, I'm not coming all the way back from deep space to sort this one out,' snapped the Professor, 'drop what you're doing and get back to London this instant. And bring the Amphora Calculosa with you.'

There was a very long pause at the Yorkshire end.

'What's the matter? Speak up Bottomley!' More silence. And even more.

'WO Bloggs sold it,' whispered The Bum, his moustache greying visibly at the thought of the impending onslaught he knew would at any moment assault his ear. The unpredictable Professor Cosmos on this occasion didn't disappoint!

'Sold it!' he yelled 'You ham-fisted bumbling idiots! What are you? What are you?'

A pause.

'Ham-fisted bumbling idiots,' mumbled The Bum.

'If Moriarty should hear of its existence the world could be in peril at any time. Get down to London with alacrity!'

'With alacrity,' whispered the General.

'I'll meet you at STOPIT HQ.'

'STOPIT,' moaned The Bum with feeling, and he wished The Brain would stop it too.

'I suppose I'll have to get you out of this mess – again – as I always do.' Saying which the immensely long-distance phone call from Professor Cosmos terminated. The General wiped the corners of his mouth with a white silk-damask table-napkin in a manner that can only be described as fatalistic. He rose from the breakfast table impressively.

'Mr Bloggs,' the General commanded quietly, 'I've decided we must return to the metropolis at once to solve this matter. Drop everything.' The Warrant Officer's jaw dropped for the second time, and a slice of toast thickly covered in honeycomb which was in his hand fell to the floor face down.

'Back to London?' He winced at the sound of his own voice. 'I've got a bit of a headache,' he whimpered feebly.

'Headache! Headache!' fumed Hycock-Bottomley, now back in double-barrelled form causing the Warrant Officer a near blackout. 'Give me the car keys and get in the back seat. Martin old boy, good to see you again; do me a favour and make my apologies to Bob and Gillie will you and explain that the safety of the world has to come before country pursuits, though I doubt if either of them will agree with my priorities. Bloggs forward!' Saying which he accelerated off to London at speed with poor Smudge groaning quietly in the back seat to soothe his agony. However, the exit was so rushed that it was the turn of the ever well-bred Augustus Hycock-Bottomley to leave a fifteen-foot skid mark in Martin's gravel drive.

If the truth were known both doughty soldiers were now feeling like very small recruits. Not only had they tried to play a cheap gag on the Professor and kid him that Martin's gallstone was a valuable antiquity; not only had they failed to spot (which the Professor had seen at once) that it was nothing less than an Amphora Calculosa; but also they'd sold it to a world-class art-collector (they thought) and it was now available to all, including Moriarty, on the open market.

'Tricky situation, sir,' whispered Bloggs.

'Indeed,' and they both fell into total silence pondering the dreadful double carpeting they would get when they got to STOPIT HQ in London. So preoccupied were they with the Professor's probable wrath, when he discovered that Bloggs had actually sold it to Moriarty, that they even forgot to stop for a cup of tea at Watford Gap.

Back at the breakfast table, Martin sat facing two boiled eggs belonging to his friends who had so hurriedly departed with their tails between their legs.

'How lucky I was feeding Tyrone his smoked salmon and didn't put my own name on that fax to the Prof,' reflected Martin. In spite of the seriousness of the situation, however, he had time to chuckle. In fact, humour, especially in bad situations, had always helped to get things into perspective. If you can manage to laugh in a desperate situation, Martin believed, it indicated you were above the situation; and if you were above the situation you stood better chance of handling it. The wit of Winston Churchill had been the secret weapon that confounded the humourless Huns. Martin reflected that the ineffectiveness of Britain's enemies had often been in direct relation to the seriousness with which they took themselves. The situation was of course very serious indeed – Moriarty was on the rampage and now most fearfully armed. Where was he? When would he strike? And at whom? The questions were unanswerable. They all now knew of the potential danger that was lurking. Martin was seriously concerned.

At that moment jockey Nick with the big grin appeared with the mail: 'Just one today Martin, and it doesn't look like a bill.'

'Thanks.' Martin opened the expensive envelope addressed in neat handwriting in black ink. Sent "EXPRESS" he noted. Inside was a visiting card which proclaimed:

WOLFGANG von MYCROFT-HOLMES
Antiquities
221B Baker Street, London
and 13 Potsdamer Platz, Berlin

Martin read on; in the bottom right hand corner were the letters PTO. He did as bid and the message on the reverse side read:

An interesting tear vase, Captain Bigglesworth: see you on September 14th with the other collectors no doubt.

September 14th? The date seemed to ring a bell... A quick glace at his William Hill complimentary diary provided the answer – he noted: *Auction at Sotheby's 10 a.m., Greco-Roman and Phoenician tear vases.*

The message on the card continued:

Perhaps we could do a deal on September 13th? Meet me at Harrods Way In Shop at 5pm, Entrance 5 and use the Lift not the Escalator. £2000 will secure.

Moriarty's endgame had clearly begun, though his strategy was still unclear. Whatever it would be, Captain Bigglesworth knew what was in the evil one's mind... the elimination of STOPIT. All his resourcefulness and courage would be demanded to the full if the tear vases of the world were not to become the receptacles of world grief.

Captain Martin Bigglesworth took comfort from the knowledge that he and his friends were at least safe until the auction at Sotheby's four days hence, enabling him, with the cool of Francis Drake in the face of the Spanish Armada, to dip another bread soldier into the General's uneaten egg.

CHAPTER 10
LOT 401A

NOTHING AT ALL happened for three days. Martin knew that Moriarty would give warning signals when he was good and ready, so he just relaxed in the garden as the weather was superb, and in the evening visited all the five pubs in Middleham – population only seven hundred as has been previously noted – and caught up with the local gossip.

So it wasn't long before the bush telegraph in the neighbouring Dales of Wensley and the river Cover had got to work and informed everyone that the eligible captain had returned and was in residence, and overnight the invitations began to arrive. His social diary was going to be as hectic as ever. How wrong so many of his London friends were who would ask him contemptuously, '…and what do you find to do up there?' Little did they know that country life is usually not only fuller but also more fulfilling than life in a big city, even the capital. M's present Yorkshire bliss was to be short-lived, however; and even as he closed his eyes for forty winks enveloped in the fragrance of an old wisteria, the phone rang.

'Captain, sir, you'll never guess,' Bloggs' voice bubbled with laughter. 'The Professor's had a note from the German, offering to sell him your gallstone.' Bloggs spluttered with hysteria. 'He's invited him to meet him. Can you guess when and where, sir?'

'The day before it goes up for sale by auction at Sotheby's. In the Way In Shop in Harrods perhaps?' suggested Martin wickedly. 'At five p.m., at Entrance Five – use the lift not the escalator?'

'You knew!' Poor Smudge was crushed.

'Of course I knew Bloggsie – I'm always a step ahead of you, remember?' (Actually that wasn't strictly true, because WO Bloggs was reputed to be one of the best Sergeants in the British Army and frequently got his Captain out of difficult situations.) 'That's why…'

'That's why you're a Captain and I'm only a WO Two,' Smudge repeated their long-standing tease, laughing.

'But you know I couldn't do without you, Smudge.' Smudge was reinflated. 'How did you know?'

'Well, it was like this, sir… The Professor received his usual complimentary copy of a Sotheby's catalogue containing details of a sale of antiquities on September 14th and out fell a compliments slip, and Herr Holmes had written on it. I've got it here – shall I read it?'

'Yes – get on with it. There may not be a second to lose.'

'Okay sir okay, keep your hair on – sorry Captain.'

'Get on with it.'

'It says: "Please refer to Lot 401A – it might interest you."'

M had already reached out for his copy of the Sotheby's catalogue – he'd noted this major sale of tear vases two days hence and was considering a trip to London to buy. Of course the prices would be astronomic but in any event the chance of meeting some of the great collectors in the field who would undoubtedly be there would have made a trip to London worthwhile even if he didn't buy anything at all. What was now puzzling him was that he couldn't find Lot 401A in his catalogue.

'Can't find it.'

'It's on a separate inserted page, sir,' – Bloggs was half a step ahead of his Captain for once – 'and guess what Lot 401A is? Your gallstone! That Kraut's making as big a fool of himself as the Prof.' Bloggs veritably hooted with laughter.

'He who laughs last…'

'What, sir? I don't get you…'

'That's why you're a Warrant Officer and I'm a Captain. Is there anything more you can tell me?'

'Er… no… just what you said… "If you are interested in a private deal on Lot 401A before the date, meet at the Way In

Shop at Harrods at five p.m. on September 13th, fifth floor, enter by door five and use the lift not the escalator. Two thousand pounds will secure."'

'The day before the sale… if we are still alive for it.' M whistled softly to himself.

Smudge was still trying to work out the quotation: 'He who laughs last…'

'…laughs longest, Smudge. This info we've got threatens the continued existence of STOPIT, not to mention the beginning of the end of life as we know it on this planet.'

M decided to go ahead with his endgame independently, however, for he had never lost sight of his secondary objective in this whole matter: to get himself reaccepted into STOPIT. He was determined to solve this latest case on his own. To M it was obvious that Moriarty was offering them the chance to buy back the Amphora Calculosa as a lure – a lure to trap the remaining members of STOPIT and bring about their death. What could be a more ignominious end that to die in a Harrods sale?

M continued mischievously: 'Do you know the difference between an elephant and a letter box, Mr Bloggs?'

'Is it a joke sir?'

'No it's serious: what's the difference?'

Bloggs thought hard: Martin could hear the cogs grinding on the phone. 'I don't know sir.'

'I won't suggest you send any more love letters to The Brain then.'

There was a pause.

'What's funny about that sir: it doesn't make sense.'

'Dear Mr Bloggs – you'll never know. Try it on The Bum,' saying which he hung up on the honest man. They were good friends, were Martin and Smudge, and they mutually respected each other's contribution to STOPIT; the teasing was all good-humoured, but really sometimes Smudge could be as thick as a strawberry milkshake.

There wasn't a moment to be lost, M knew that, but first he had to do some cool, hard thinking – no sense charging off to London before his revised plan was clear in his mind. He put on some hiking boots and climbed to the top of Penn Hill, carefully following the narrow sheep tracks so as not to disturb the grouse. He started up several birds lucky enough to have escaped an explosive death at the wrong end of the General's Purdies three days earlier thanks to the breakfast phone call of Professor Cosmos which had summoned them immediately back to London. The view towards Wensleydale from the cairn at the top of Penn Hill was breathtaking: over six hundred feet above sea level and you could see the edge of the Yorkshire Moors and the rolling Cleveland hills some twenty-five miles away to the east. Scarborough and a view of the sea was of course beyond, slightly to the left of Cleveland range as he looked from his vantage point: the dominating feature in this part of the Pennines. Further to the north he could see the myriad of chimneys and rigs in the poisoned haze over Middlesbrough, permanently expanding its polluting pall of chemical emissions.

'When will Britain do the right thing and put clean air before profit?' he mused, reflecting on the lack of fish even in his little river Cover because of the chemicals greedy farmers were encouraged to use to overproduce, and overfeed the overfed. However, there wasn't time to ponder any more on matters green; he must allow the great feeling of superiority and freedom of mind offered by this truly great view of the Dales to inspire a solution to the case that might, with justification, now be called Operation H.A.T.E.!

M went over the new facts in his mind. The Professor had been invited, and he too was being enticed, by Moriarty to meet him at five p.m. at the Way In Shop in Harrods (which was on the fifth floor) entering by Entrance Five. First – was there any significance in the repetition of the figure five, or was it just whimsy? No immediate answer came to mind, so M let a metaphoric hook dangle in his cranium so that any passing brainwave might be caught. What else? 'Use the lift, not the escalator…' That must be significant – but why? Again no immediate solution; another metaphoric hook. 'Two thousand pounds will secure' – well that was easy; that was nothing: just Moriarty's inept attempt to make the enticement look genuine.

M descended the hill slowly, thinking. By the time he got back to Hepple House, nature's rush hour had begun. The rooks were settling in noisily for the night in the great elms that surrounded Middleham House with which he shared a very high stone wall. Starlings were wheeling in their thousands; soon the owl would fly across the square with a soft hoot, in deference to the little hill town's Cross it seemed, as was its nocturnal wont. More important to M at this moment was that the whole planet of men, women and children were unaware of their fate that was drawing ever closer. It was clear that Moriarty intended to lure the four of them to Harrods and eliminate them; he just needed them to know who was the real Master of the World first before finishing them off, otherwise it wouldn't be any fun – for him. Death, destruction and despair: these to Moriarty were as a teddy to a baby: comforts, playthings.

A plan was forming in the brave Captain's mind... YES! He knew what to do!

Quickly he packed his essentials into a sports bag. These included a three-generations-old but super quality and still-smart dinner-jacket with a plum-red silk lining which had belonged to the father of a famous old thespian and been given to him when he was an impoverished young cadet at Sandhurst and the ageing star was clearing out his Castlenau wardrobe.

'Well, it won't all be business in London: I'm sure I can fit a little pleasure in too.' Thinking which, he added to his packing list a bottle of Trumper's Curzon aftershave, a diamond tie-pin, a silver twizzle stick (he never liked too many bubbles in his Dom Perignon), a white monogrammed silk scarf and an extra pair of Calvin Kleins. In five minutes the bag was packed.

However, before he left he slipped something into his left sock: it was his trusty little PPK which he'd conveniently omitted to hand in and on which the Quartermaster had turned an uncharacteristically blind eye.

He went downstairs for a quick snack before his long drive south. He advanced on the fridge. No alcohol because he was driving, so he poured himself a glass of cold milk and tucked into a generous slice of game pie which had been The Bum and

Smudge's arrival present a few days before; ironically they'd bought it at Harrods.

'I think there's time for some raspberries and cream too.' Fresh coffee bubbling on the AGA soon found its way into a Georgian silver coffee pot and he relaxed into his great-grandfather's wing chair by the fire.

Eight fifty-five p.m. and his last moment of relaxation was over. His sporting little MGB was allowed to rest in a barn and M slid out of the drive of Hepple House in his classic silver Mercedes 450 SLC which was more suited to long journeys. Night was already falling in the Dales and his great sports saloon, Mercedes' flagship model of the time, headed for London almost without instruction and, it must be said, at an unrecorded speed.

'No time to waste,' M murmured to himself as he joined the fast lane of the M1; 'the future of mankind may be at stake.'

M was on the trail.

CHAPTER 11
DEATH AT HARRODS

AT FIVE FIFTY-FIVE a.m. the next morning, after a speed-of-light three-and-three-quarter-hour drive to his London flat, and five and a quarter hour's sound sleep, M was awakened by his "barking dog" alarm clock. Five minutes' wake-up time and he was fully conscious, and on cue the bells of Westminster Cathedral struck the hour of six. M's Doomsday had begun: the day which might well prove to be his last on earth. His last? Yes – because the only scenario M could see that had any chance of succeeding required the ultimate sacrifice from him. Failure was certain death for humanity; success for humanity… it had to be done. A brave and selfless decision.

Timing was one of Captain Martin Bigglesworth's strong points, and in order to pull off the plan he had formulated in his mind since receiving Warrant Officer Bloggs' phone call the previous night, the most precise timing would be needed. Showered, with Molton Brown's Eucalyptus, and breakfasted – porridge with cream and soft brown sugar, lightly scrambled egg, two Nairn's rough oatmeal biscuits with honeycomb, half a slice of brown toast and home-made marmalade (made by him) and a pot of Darjeeling leaf tea – and M was ready for action, ready to write the last chapter in the epic single-handed make-or-break mission of Captain Martin Bigglesworth to challenge evil and to regain entry to the elite STOPIT unit. He wouldn't be eating again for some time: perhaps this was his last meal.

Was this the final chapter too for the teeming billions innocently toiling and spinning on the surface of the good planet Earth? Bigglesworth contemplated the garish campanile of Westminster Cathedral from the window of his aunt's flat in Ashley Gardens. Was he exaggerating the importance of his single-handed mission? Frankly, no. At five p.m. that very evening the world would hold its breath if it knew the spider-thin thread on which its little planet would be dangling.

The antiquated mahogany and brass lift was now at street level as M stepped out into the early morning sunshine. Westminster Abbey distantly and the Catholic Cathedral a hundred yards away announced in agreement the hour of eight. He entered the Cathedral and lit a candle and knelt for a few silent minutes. Back in the street a few early-bird shops were opening and the air still had a tinge of freshness as he crossed Victoria Street and walked on down side roads towards St James's Park. Before starting his day of action proper he popped into Bircham and Co, his solicitors in Dean Farrar Street, to make his will... A take-away coffee in his hand, he sat for half an hour beside the Serpentine going over his detailed plans in his head.

As he crossed the park now towards the castellations of St James' Palace you may wonder why our hero had got up so early and after so little sleep when his confrontation with Moriarty wouldn't be until five p.m. that evening. Firstly, he only ever slept five and a half hours; and secondly he had things to do...

Up to this morning he'd prepared himself in mind and body for his ordeal – now he was heading for a little arcade of Georgian shops in St James Street behind Lock's, his hatters'. Had he been followed (he hadn't been: he'd checked on that, his training never forgotten) any followers would have been mystified to see M disappear into an exclusive theatrical costumiers! M's preparations would ensure that his five p.m. "death or glory" encounter at Harrods was to be a triumph of Oscar-winning detail and finesse, and also, it has to be admitted, a slight indulgence to his thespian inclinations.

Let's recap: the object of the mission was to repossess the Amphora Calculosa – with or without the MMG itself – and preferably without loss of life; imagination as well as courage was essential. The apprehending and permanent neutralising of Moriarty himself, though a desirable bonus, was realistically not M's priority. 'Pigs might fly,' he thought, 'but I've never seen one do so. Let's just save the world from immediate and long-term threat.' It was clear that at, or shortly after, five p.m. this very evening, if the Amphora Calculosa hadn't been recovered, the outlook for mankind would be black and bleak indeed.

Mission completed at the costumiers, our Captain reappeared with a huge and exciting-looking dark green plastic sack, a classy hat box and a pink feather boa round his neck, which clearly he hadn't been able to squash into the bag or box. (Or perhaps he just liked wearing it!) A chauffeur-driven Addison-Lee car was waiting for him and he climbed in saying: 'Yes, it's 56 Davies Street, driver, if you please.'

Now 56 Davies Street, just round the corner from Claridges, is the HQ of the Officers Club of a very exclusive crack TA Regiment: the Queen Victoria's Rifles. He had served with the Green Jackets (now known as The Rifles) and on leaving to go to university he had joined their TA regiment; then STOPIT had head-hunted him. No time for lunch here in the mess and even one Gin and French would affect his aim! So he settled for a tonic water.

Around four p.m. he left for his appointment with Fate at his Knightsbridge apotheosis… leaving some of his regimental friends still *bon viveur*-ing in this Mayfair oasis. It should be noted that he was not sporting the pink feather boa!

It was a late opening at Harrods and the store was busy. It was one minute to five and there was no sign of either the good or the evil protagonists in this bizarre drama. Fifty-nine seconds later as the clocks were preparing to strike the hour a London black cab pulled up at Entrance Five; out stepped three men. The first to emerge was Professor Cosmos who looked as if he'd just got out of bed and didn't appear to have any money when the driver looked expectantly at him, so the second, an erect figure in an immaculately cut grey flannel suit and suede brogues which would have done credit to any a ducal foot, stepped into the breach proffering a truly crumpled fifty-pound note (which he'd probably won off a bookie at Lingfield the previous Saturday). This simply elicited expletives from the cabbie and remarks about not having change, which could have been heard from Tattersalls to the Brompton Oratory. The erect figure, whom you've no doubt guessed was none other than General Augustus Hycock-Bottomley in mufti, turned instantly to the hapless Bloggs who was made to turn out all his pockets for small change for the cab.

'Chop-chop man! It's 1700 hours!'

Of Moriarty there was no sign at all; our hero, though watching, was inconspicuous.

The performance of paying for the taxi over, the three members of STOPIT approached Door Five. As if by magic the door was opened by discreet commissionaires and the three crossed the threshold into the world's most famous – and today most dangerous – department store.

'Where the devil's Bigglesworth?' demanded the General.

'I told you he was unreliable,' growled the irascible Professor.

'Can't wait for him – we go ahead with the RV,' the General commanded and made to stride for the escalator, but Bloggs restrained him.

'"Use the lift, not the escalator", remember sir?'

The escalator was to the right; the shoppers who were using it appeared to be mentally switched off and, with vacant expressions and arms full of expensive-looking parcels, were allowing themselves to be sedately transported up or down. The lift lay directly ahead: more correctly the twin lift. One was an express one and went directly up to the Way In Shop on the fifth floor; the other called in at Lingerie, Antiques, Bathrooms and the Zoo before hitting the trendy boutique. The three changed course, but you could see the General wasn't pleased to have been corrected in front of the Professor. They paused at the lift, and an untrained observer would not have noticed the momentary exchange of glances between the three. As their eyes met for the briefest of seconds, they each read in the others' expressions a message of encouragement and, just in case, farewell. Imperceptibly – unless of course one were sharp enough of eye to see it – they took a deep breath and the General lent forward to press the impressive bell to summon the lift. The doors of the lift opened and an immaculately turned-out lift man stepped out.

'Step in,' he commanded with chilling intensity. The lift man had a sallow skin like wax, black hair and neatly trimmed black moustache and beard. His eyes, if they could have been seen behind the dark glasses he was wearing, were slimy as a slug's belly, jet black and of unfathomable profundity…

At that second the doors of the second lift – the express lift – opened, and an equally well turned-out lift man emerged – and it was none other than Captain Martin Bigglesworth!

'Get into mine!' he commanded.

Shocked by his tone but not needing any explanations as, out of habit and training, trusting the Bigglesworth they knew of old, the three bundled themselves in and M quickly closed the doors behind them. A group of American shoppers wanting the lift man to take them to Bath Towels on the second floor were much surprised when this deferential Harrods employee pushed the first in line in the stomach with such fiendish force that they all fell back into the lobby on top of each other like a heap of discarded dominoes, the lift ascending without them. One blue-rinsed woman with a pampered poodle was so cross she said she wouldn't bring her children to see Father Christmas ever again.

The Captain's express lift had accelerated upstairs so fast that the STOPIT trio were thrown to the floor in a pile with Smudge on the bottom, his stomach having remained at street level. M explained rapidly:

'We'll get to the fifth floor first because Moriarty's lift will stop at every floor.' Little did he know of the rude ejection of the Americans, nor of the speed of Moriarty's lift. He continued: 'As soon as we get to the top, you, General, take cover behind the racks of Tweeds from The Highlands you'll spot in front of you and slightly to the right; Mr Bloggs slightly to the left as you step out you'll see a rack of Baby Doll Night Dresses – hide behind them; Professor Cosmos stand innocently, as Moriarty instructed in his letter, looking at your watch or something, precisely in the centre of the space as you step out of the lift – I've marked the exact spot on the floor with a small cross of gaffer tape. We need to have Moriarty

78

completely covered when his lift arrives just seconds after we do.'

'And you...?' began The Brain – but he got no answer from M as the lift had arrived at the fifth floor. M opened the doors. Bloggs and the General were out first with a speed and agility that rightly made STOPIT the toast of British Combined Forces and disappeared into Tweeds and Baby Doll Dresses as instructed. The Brain followed, every inch as cool as a cucumber, or as one arriving precisely on time for a business appointment. M, sporting his disguise as a Harrods lift man (provided with other items from the theatrical costumiers that morning), was the last of the team to leave the lift as the doors closed automatically behind him...

...but Moriarty suddenly appeared from behind Bespoke Evening Wear and to their horror confronted them! He had got there first! Having jettisoned his passengers at street level, and bypassed The Bra Bar, Bureaux, Bidets and Border Collies, he was standing facing them framed by designer labels.

'Very clever Captain Bigglesworth, but not quite clever enough: your lift may have been zee express lift, but mine vas not a lift at all! I arranged for my lift to be removed for repairs this morning and replaced it vis my Time Capsule vich filled zee lift-shaft exactly. Bad luck, do you say? *Schweinhunden!*' He spoke with a heavy German accent.

For only the second time in his life Captain Bigglesworth looked crestfallen.

Although not afraid to die himself, he was fearful of the fate from which he had failed to save his friends, and the world catastrophe that would inevitably follow. Not all the tear vases in the world would be enough to contain just one tear from every mortal who would now suffer. The prospect was too terrible to contemplate. He turned with profound apology to his colleagues:

'General...' he began.

'Not your fault, Bigglesworth; as a matter of fact your planning and execution were quite exceptional and your strategic thinking most imaginative.'

'I wouldn't have guessed, Martin, so how could you?' added The Brain, but he didn't mean to sound so arrogant. Bloggs put a manly hand on the Captain's shoulder.

Moriarty, looking like the cat who'd got the cream and the goldfish from the fish tank as well, abruptly ordered them to step back into his false lift, then drew a deep and smugly satisfied breath and began a valedictory speech he'd been working on for a number of years and had been longing to deliver to his hated foes. In fact they'd cheated him of his chances to read this speech so many times that the pages had turned brown and started to curl up at the corners. He began:

'In a few moments you vill all be eliminated!!! Your lift vill crash six floors into zee basement Hairdressing Department: and zis vill give you zee closest shave you never had because it vill be CURTAINS FOR YOU!!!'

He laughed a wild, terrifying and maniacal laugh and, snorting with contempt, the cruel Moriarty continued:

'Zee close shave vas a gut joke. *Nicht war*? Zee good in zee vorld vill be viped out at a stroke, and uzzer forces vill have unfettered reign.' He chuckled very slightly and most unpleasantly at the prospect, but a terrible frisson ran down the spines of his four listeners. This man meant business: his were no idle threats. 'I must apologise,' he continued, 'for dragging you down to London to zis vonce delightful corner shop, but it seemed such a vimsical place to encounter each uzzer for zee last time – and also I do have to purchase a few new ties. Furzermore I couldn't exterminate you – lovely vord "exterminate" if I may borrow zee terminology from an ugly but useful past colleague of mine – vizout allowing myself zee pleasure of knowing zat you knew who had "done it". I also felt I should like you to know how much I have admired you as adversaries.' That was big of him, thought Bloggs. 'You have indeed nearly trimmed my beard for me several times and caused me several problems. But zen Vimbledon is only fun ven all zee players are champions, don't you agree? Zis time zough...' (and the tennis metaphor had just given Moriarty a neat way to conclude his oration in a rather witty and totally original way – he thought – so he actually smiled very slightly) 'Zis time,' he repeated himself for greater emphasis. 'Zis time, it is game, set and match... to *me!*' and he raised his MMG to eliminate STOPIT and send them minimised, mushed and minced and crashing to their doom in Hairdressing...

Without a moment's hesitation Captain Martin Bigglesworth, that unbelievably brave young officer, calmly stepped forward.

'Very interesting, Wolfy, but there's just one little thing that's going to oblige you to have to throw away that pretty little speech into the nearest dustbin and start again. In fact I'll write it for you if you like,' he offered helpfully. Moriarty's finger hovered in the MMG's applicator and he looked outraged. 'And you can drop that pathetic German accent disguise: it fools nobody. You see, Wolfy,' M continued somewhat cheekily, 'I made a pottery copy of your Amphora Calculosa – I did life and sculpture classes at Oxford, did you know, so I'm handy with both clay and curvaceous objects – and it is that copy, and not the actual Amphora Calculosa that transforms the toy in your hand to a lethal weapon, that's in your MMG now.'

And as M, with the cool of the driest Gin and French this side of South Carolina, stretched out his hand for the MMG, Moriarty momentarily glanced down in horror to check. In that split second M leapt forward like a cougar from the bush, and knocked the MMG flying out of Moriarty's hand, to be lost in a flurry of tulle hanging on a rail marked "Petticoats 4 Popsies". Moriarty himself sidestepped, however, and left the Captain sprawling on the floor like a rug. Taking this as his cue to depart, and leaping over Martin who lay spread-eagled from Gucci to Armani, Moriarty made his escape towards his "lift". He was thwarted, however, by a matronly lady, the massive size of whose bosoms were matched only by her colossal handbag with which she swiped him: Moriarty fell like a stone to the ground (there was in fact a brick inside the bag) and instantly the matron was on top of him.

'What's going on?' queried a stunned Bloggs who emerged from a collection of summer dresses cleverly disguised as Shirley Temple in a pink gingham frock.

'Help her!' ordered the General who was wearing a sporran but no kilt. But the matronly shopper needed no help – for from behind counters, mannequins and unseen corners in the Way In Shop had sprung a complete platoon (or so it seemed) of debs, porters and sales staff, bedecked in costumes M had hired from the Theatrical Costumiers that morning, and in no time at all Moriarty had been trussed up like a spring chicken. The matron rose with a satisfied grin (matched only by M's) and removed her disguise which would have made Aretha Franklin look like a twig insect. It was none other than Corporal Smith; and, as the debs, porters and sales staff removed their disguises too, The Brain, the General and the Warrant Officer were astonished to see the whole of Number One Platoon, A Company of Special Terrestrial Operations Project Intelligence Taskforce.

'Well done!' said Professor Cosmos.

'Thank you Captain!' said the General.

'Cor streuth!' said WO Bloggs, who emerged spinning the MMG (containing the now-known-to-be-a-pottery-copy dummy Amphora Calculosa), which he'd retrieved from under a pile of ladies' smalls, nonchalantly on his index finger cowboy-style. There was a spontaneous round of applause from everyone... except M who yelled at Bloggs:

'*Freeze!*'

Bloggs froze at the urgency of his Captain's command. M gently approached him and whispered quietly: 'Give me the MMG, it's armed.'

You could have heard a pin drop; it was as if everyone had stopped breathing.

'It's not a pottery copy,' said the Captain quietly, 'it's the real thing.'

CHAPTER 12

CUCUMBER SANDWICHES

SITTING RELAXED IN Harrods Silver Restaurant half an hour later, Captain Martin Bigglesworth was placing an order with a waitress:

'Four slices of Victoria Sponge and a large pot of Lapsang Souchong tea please.'

There was a warm and comfortable pause as Warrant Officer Bloggs, Professor Cosmos and the General gazed with speechless admiration at our understated hero. It was the General who broke the silence.

'So the Amphora Calculosa in Moriarty's MMG wasn't a pottery copy at all?'

'No, General – it was the real thing.' The implications of this knowledge were of course truly staggering. It took a few moments to sink in.

'You were just bluffing to Moriarty then?' gasped an adulating Warrant Officer. 'The MMG Moriarty was pointing at us was fully armed and lethal all the time?'

With characteristic modesty and Yorkshire economy of language Martin replied: 'Yes.'

'That was a brave thing to do, Martin,' said the Professor.

'I'm proud of you, Colonel,' said the General.

'Well done, Colonel, sir!' said the Warrant Officer – and allowed himself the familiarity of a wink at his friend.

'All in the course of a day's… what!!' The former Captain came to a shocked halt mid sentence as he realised how the General and then his WO Two had addressed him.

'Colonel? Did you say "Colonel", General Augustus?'

'You're reinstated into STOPIT, Martin – and as a Colonel. STOPIT will be recommending you to Her Majesty the Queen for a Victoria Cross in due course. You risked your life in the service of your Country and the world population.'

Martin simply lost his power of speech for a moment.

'Thank you. Thank you,' he managed to say eventually.

'As a matter of fact you'd never left,' added the General with a twinkle in his eye. He turned to the Professor: 'Will you explain or shall I?'

'Go ahead General; he's your department.'

'Well, Martin, never for a moment did we seriously doubt your ability to serve with STOPIT, but your undoubted setback with the Pink Laser gave us the utterly convincing excuse we needed to get you into plain clothes and working under cover.'

A look of sheer astonishment passed over M's face.

'You see, Martin, we desperately needed an undercover agent because Intelligence told us that Moriarty was within an ace of a development which would clinch his world mastery. We couldn't simply import an agent because your background goes back so far; and anyway no one, however well briefed, could do this investigatory job as convincingly as you: after all you are rather a good actor.'

'Investigator – and bait!' interjected M ruefully.

'Yes, I'm afraid so Martin: we risked your life for you. I hope you won't feel we've let you down – put you through unnecessary stress.'

'Let me down? I'm honoured to have been chosen to have been of such service to STOPIT and to my Country. I just can't tell you...' He couldn't continue.

'To continue,' said the General, 'Moriarty had to believe you were as good as dead so far as STOPIT's activities were concerned. The experiments Moriarty was involved with this time, concerned as they were with the use of the rare Moroccan Spitting Snake for the transference of a deadly stone-producing bacterium, were of exceptional interest.'

'I could use the knowledge myself: I've always wanted an Amphora Calculosa,' interjected the Professor under his breath. The General continued:

'The essential final test had of course to be on a human. If ex-Captain Martin Bigglesworth (deliberately by chance, if you see what I mean) was allowed to cross his path, it would indeed from Moriarty's viewpoint be killing two birds with one stone: he'd get his Amphora Calculosa and the guinea pig which by happy chance (as he thought) would be you. From our point of view too, to use you Bigglesworth was killing two birds with one stone as we were able to stop Moriarty's final achievement and also finally to prove your fitness for duty.'

'Which you never doubted anyway,' interjected Martin wickedly; the General and The Brain looked a little uncomfortable.

'Supposing the idea of belly dancers in Morocco hadn't attracted me and I'd settled on an Under-30s Club holiday in a sarong of shells instead? You'd have been up the creek I fear.'

'Ah!' said The Bum and The Brain together.

'You tell him General.'

'No – you tell him Professor.'

'I'll tell him,' said Smudge. 'It was like this Martin... er Colonel, sir... er.'

'Martin'll do tonight, Bloggsie.' They were good friends of long standing.

'Well, it was like this...' And WO Bloggs, with prompting from the others, amazed Martin by the revelation that even before the Seven-Legged Arachnoids had been hobbled, STOPIT intelligence had got wind of Moriarty's Amphora Calculosa research and secret tests.

The General piped up: 'A counter-strategy was worked out, and now after nearly four years of tense and taxing work with STOPIT, it was totally credible that the demands of STOPIT could have left your nerves frayed and in genuine need of a holiday to stave off a nervous breakdown so...'

'But I was fit as a flea,' M interjected.

'That was the whole point,' explained The Brain. 'You were indeed as fit as a flea – but you might easily not have been, and our counter-espionage had no difficulty in infiltrating the idea to Moriarty's undercover slaves (LA Zac and Swansea David) that you were on the edge of a major nervous crisis. So by retiring you from STOPIT, Moriarty would never guess that you were actually still very much on STOPIT's active service.'

'My idea,' beamed The Bum. 'Had to box clever.'

'Good one wasn't it?' beamed Smudge.

'Mmm – very,' M agreed, beginning to understand what they'd been up to.

'So,' continued the General, 'knowing that Moriarty had developed the technology to grow his Amphora Calculosa (and thus be able to activate an MMG) by implanting it in a human gall bladder, we also needed to know where he would strike so we could track him, and eventually eliminate him; so I decided…'

'…so I suggested we send you off to Morocco to have a mind-blowing experience with the Gnouia belly dancers in Morocco,' chirped in Smudge. 'Neat idea wasn't it? I knew you'd fall for the birds! "One Gnouia in the hand is worth two Noras in a sarong," that's always been your motto, hasn't it sir?'

'I'm telling this story, Mr Bloggs,' said the General, who'd been enjoying holding the stage. 'So I rang you to suggest a holiday in Morocco to find the Gnouia belly dancers knowing you'd fall for… knowing you'd be interested in the historical antecedents of Gnouia dancing…'

'Why phone? Wasn't that a bit of a security risk? I haven't got any scramble device on my phone.'

'Precisely! I phoned you in Yorkshire because we knew that Moriarty had learnt the dark art of phone-tapping when he was working for a scurrilous mass-circulation newspaper as a journalist in London. Listening in to us he'd know exactly where to find you…'

'Thanks,' M said with some irony.

'And he did,' concluded the General, ever one to state the obvious.

'So we could trap him,' added Bloggs with relish.

'What we didn't know' – now it was The Brain who took up the story – 'was that Moriarty had already infiltrated one of LA Zac's amazing WHITHER SCIENCE TODAY? Conventions in Los Angeles, hypnotised Zac, got him to phone you, and… well the rest is history.'

'Was that nice Welsh guy one of Moriarty's gang?'

'Yes – they picked David up on a wet night in Swansea.'

'What was Moriarty doing in Swansea?'

'No idea: must have got his coordinates in a twist.'

'So there you are,' concluded the General. 'Colonel Martin Bigglesworth rides with honour. You came up trumps for reliability, judgement and courage, so you've got your promotion.'

'And I've got a nine-inch gallbladder scar across my stomach like the aftermath of a shark attack to prove it!' M commented with a note of mock-complaint in his voice.

'Let's have a look!' goofed Smudge.

'Decorum, decorum, WO One.'

'What?' gasped Bloggs.

'I said "decorum".'

'No – after that – you called me "WO One": I'm a WO Two sir.'

'Not any more, Mr Bloggs – I've promoted you,' said the new Colonel.

Bloggs blushed.

'Thank you, sir.'

They shook hands. Then Bloggs, in his euphoria forgetting himself, reached for the last cucumber sandwich on the plate – but the Colonel got there first.

'Sorry Mr Bloggs – rank still has its perks!'

'So everyone's happy,' said Professor Cosmos, 'and I'm off!'

Mission accomplished! And that's how Martin Bigglesworth was reunited with his friends and colleagues – but the story doesn't end there...

'Here's to STOPIT's next engagement lads... tomorrow morning 0900 hours.' The General was in his most commanding mood. 'It'll be a nasty business: are you up for it Colonel?'

But Colonel Martin Bigglesworth – familiarly known as M – was unable to answer immediately as his mouth was still full of a certain cucumber sandwich; so the General had to wait a polite moment for the answer to his question.

Cucumber sandwich consumed, Colonel Martin smiled broadly and said:

'I'm up for anything!'

ABOUT THE AUTHOR
RICHARD FRANKLIN

RICHARD FRANKLIN HAS published three poems, five well-received plays (one of which, *The Cage* on homelessness, won an Edinburgh Fringe Festival Award) and numerous articles for magazines, play reviews and politico/philosophical tracts. In demand as an actor, with an exceptional speaking and recording voice, Richard is also an experienced theatre director.

Operation H.A.T.E. is Richard's first novella, and while it is a work of total fiction it draws on his background in Berkshire, London and Yorkshire and his experiences on a visit to Morocco he made when he was an undergraduate at Oxford. Richard is best known to the public all over the English-speaking world as Captain Mike Yates of U.N.I.T., a role he created and played for nearly four years in the iconic BBC TV series *Doctor Who*, in the classic Jon Pertwee era.